Mean Margaret

Mean Margaret

Tor Seidler

Pictures by **Jon Agee**

Laura Geringer Books

HarperTrophy®
An Imprint of HarperCollinsPublishers

HarperTrophy® is a registered trademark of HarperCollins Publishers Inc.

Mean Margaret
Text copyright © 1997 by Tor Seidler
Pictures copyright © 1997 by Jon Agee

Library of Congress Cataloging-in-Publication Data
Seidler, Tor.
    Mean Margaret / Tor Seidler ; pictures by Jon Agee.
        p.   cm.
    ISBN 0-06-205090-7 — ISBN 0-06-441039-0 (pbk.)
    [1. Behavior—Fiction.   2. Toddlers—Fiction.]   I. Title.   II. Agee, Jon, ill.
PZ7.S45526 Me   1997   97-71566
[Fic]—dc21   CIP
                                                                                            AC

Typography by Steve Scott
❖
First HarperTrophy edition, 2001

Visit us on the World Wide Web!
www.harperchildrens.com

For Holly McGhee

Contents

Mean Margaret

A Cold Shoulder

One spring afternoon Fred was out foraging for food in the meadow when an inky cloud seeped over the sun. He was a good ways from his burrow—nearly to the pig farm, judging by the whiff of the sloppy beasts he'd just caught. Since there was nothing he hated more than getting his fur wet, Fred scampered up into a hole in a maple by the roadside. This required little effort—woodchucks are distant relatives of squirrels—but the hole was a dreadful mess.

"Woodpeckers," Fred muttered.

When he poked his head out to look for something better, he was momentarily blinded by a flash of lightning. Then he was nearly deafened by a clap of thunder, and right after that a violent cracking sound set his very bones vibrating.

Seconds later, the skies opened.

"Of all the rotten luck," Fred said.

Stuck, Fred passed the time complaining about the filthy habits of woodpeckers. "Don't they know what a broom is . . ." Being a woodchuck who lived alone, he often talked to himself. But he turned silent when a pair of fat, ugly human beings came running in under the tree.

"Goodness!" said the woman.

"We're soaked to the skin," said the man, who had a big ham under his arm.

Fred held his nose. The odor of the human beings' wet clothing wasn't much better than the whiff of pig he'd gotten earlier.

"You know, Mr. Hubble," the woman said after a while, "this really isn't so bad, is it?"

"Nice break from the kids," the man agreed.

Eventually the rain stopped and the sun returned, scattering the meadow with diamonds of light. But, to the woodchuck's dismay, the fat, smelly people stayed put.

"Look, Mrs. Hubble," the man said. "A rainbow."

"Where?"

"There—right over the pigsty."

"Oh, my, yes. How beautiful!"

Fred noticed the rainbow, too. However, it was small comfort to him. For now Mr. Hubble put his free arm around Mrs. Hubble's middle, and Mrs. Hubble leaned her head on Mr. Hubble's shoulder.

"Good grief," Fred said under his breath. "I'm going to be here forever."

But rainbows rarely last very long, and when this one faded away, Mrs. Hubble let out a sigh and said, "I suppose we better head back. They'll be turning the place upside down."

As soon as the Hubbles waddled off down the road, Fred evacuated the nasty hole. He'd never been happier to get home—though, even so, he didn't forget to wipe his feet thoroughly just inside the entrance mound. He took great pride in his burrow. It was the tidiest, most private place imaginable. Digging it had been the low point of his life— nothing soiled your paws like digging—but at least he would never have to go through that horror again. He'd gritted his teeth and dug extra deep, ensuring that he would never be subjected to the creeping of centipedes or the squawking of blue jays. The only time he was ever disturbed was when a certain striped snake chased some prey down his bolt hole. And this was only a minor annoyance, since the snake was a creature of few words—even when his mouth wasn't full of frog or mouse.

Climbing the maple had mussed up Fred's fur, so the first thing he did was carefully clean and brush himself.

Then he sat down in his favorite armchair, the one by his jar of glowworms, and recovered from his ordeal, basking in the neatness, the dryness, the luxurious peace of his home. Instead of the glare of lightning, there was the soft glow of the worms. Instead of smelly human beings, there was the pleasant fragrance of his pine furniture. And instead of bone-vibrating cracks, there was sublime silence. He didn't hear a single sound till his own stomach began to growl.

Fred padded into his kitchen and fixed himself a special treat: three snails on a bed of clover. After dinner, he began to feel pleasantly drowsy, and once he'd cleaned up the kitchen, he covered the glowworms with a leaf, crept into his bedroom, and snuggled into bed. He said his prayers, thanking heaven for giving him everything a woodchuck could possibly want, and closed his eyes.

The bed was nice and warm, so when a shiver went through him, he sat up in surprise. "Could I have caught cold in that miserable tree?" he asked himself. "It *was* damp." He swallowed. "My throat's not sore, though."

Fred checked himself for swollen glands. None. The

only thing out of the ordinary was a slight chill in his shoulder. He lay back down, burying his chilly shoulder under the covers. Suddenly he was a married woodchuck, with a wife who warmed his shoulder by leaning her head on it.

Fred woke up in alarm.

"Whew," he said, realizing he was alone. "What a terrible dream!"

In the morning the dream seemed the height of silliness. "A wife, what a ridiculous idea," he said as he did his sweeping. "How could you keep things just so with another woodchuck around?"

But come evening, the chill crept into his shoulder again, and that night the same dream woke him in the small hours. It became a nightly ritual—a nightly *torture* for a woodchuck who hated having his routine disturbed as much as Fred did. He tried everything he could think of: sleeping on his back, cutting out strong foods like mint and dandelion greens, counting field mice. But nothing helped. Time and again he sat bolt upright in his bed in the middle of the night, shuddering from the dream of being married.

Greenhouse Blues

Woodchucks will nibble nearly any plant, but most of them are partial to vegetables, and at this time of year—it was April—the only place in Fred's neighborhood where vegetables were readily available was the greenhouse across the meadow. Early in the morning, before the arrival of the gardener, this greenhouse was a very popular woodchuck gathering place. But Fred never went near it. He liked to sleep till nine, and besides, he hated exposing his fur to morning dew. Furthermore, he wasn't crazy about mixing with others.

Still, the greenhouse was the obvious spot for wife-hunting, and after being plagued by his dream every night for over a week, Fred was desperate enough to try anything. He didn't really want a mate, of course. But if he went through the motions of looking for one, maybe the nightmare would leave him alone and life would return to normal.

When the dream woke him for the tenth time, he

dragged himself out of his cozy bed and up to his entrance mound. "You've lost your mind, Fred," he said bluntly, staring into the chilly darkness. All he could make out was the white bark of a nearby birch tree. But he forced himself on, devising a greenhouse strategy as he felt his way along. If he spotted a potential wife there, he would go up to her and say, "Excuse me for disturbing you, but I was wondering if you could direct me to the beans . . ."

By the time Fred was halfway across the meadow, he was dew-drenched. But the sun was poking up over the horizon, and once he reached the greenhouse, he went over to the east side and positioned himself on a rock so that the sun's rays hit his right side directly and bounced off the greenhouse glass to toast his left. When he was reasonably dry, he gave his fur a quick once-over and followed the scent of his fellow woodchucks behind a shrub and through a missing glass pane.

Though comfortably warm, the greenhouse was a bit humid for Fred's taste. But as he made his way around some rather noxious-smelling marigolds, he spotted an attractive female woodchuck over by a row of peas.

"Excuse me for disturbing you," he said, going up to her, "but I was wondering if you could direct me to the beans."

The female looked surprised. "Why?"

"Well, I thought I might sample one."

"But the beans are so stringy. Try one of these." She held out a pawful of peas.

"Um, no thanks." It was too early for breakfast, and besides, he liked to wash his food before eating it.

"Oh, go on," she said, popping a couple of peas into her mouth. "They're yummy."

She smiled as she chewed, to show how delicious they were. But all Fred saw was her pea-green teeth. She chewed with her mouth open!

He was so disgusted he slipped out of the greenhouse and went straight home. But that night the chill snuck back into his shoulder, and the same dream disturbed his slumber. So he went through the whole ordeal again: dragging himself out of bed and across the sodden meadow, drying himself on the rock, slipping into the muggy greenhouse.

This time he made his way over to the carrots. Carrots were said to be "brain food"; maybe there he would find a woodchuck intelligent enough to chew with her mouth closed. And, indeed, he saw a very appealing-looking female crouched among the carrot tops.

"Excuse me for disturbing you, but I was wondering if you could direct me to the beans."

"Green, wax, or lima?" she asked with a friendly smile.

"Green, I guess," he said, noting her sparkling teeth.

"I believe they're over there, under the second-to-last sprinkler head." She stood up on her hind legs and pointed—with the filthiest front paw he'd ever seen. Of course, she'd been digging for carrots, but still . . .

"That does it," Fred muttered on the trek home. "No more getting up before dawn for this woodchuck."

But the bad dream continued to haunt him, and he eventually resorted to giving the greenhouse a third try. This time he weaved his way into the far end, where the sugar beets grew. Turning between two rows of them, he spied a woodchuck with the sweetest smile he'd ever seen. The closer he got, however, the clearer it was that she had a sweet tooth as well. She completely filled the furrow. In fact, she was over twice his size.

This distressing experience put him off the greenhouse for several days. But the dream persisted, and he ended up going back again and again. Every female he met was flawed. If she was a good conversationalist, her fur was every which way. If her fur was well-groomed, she didn't take care of her teeth.

"It's hopeless," he finally decided. "I'll just have to live with a chilly shoulder." So he returned to his old routine of getting up at nine, eating a civilized breakfast, and cleaning house.

One day, while he was dusting, the striped snake burst into his living room. "Brown toad come through here?" the snake asked.

Fred shook his head, and the snake turned to leave. But instead of letting him go, as he usually would have, Fred cleared his throat and said, "Snake?"

"Yeah?"

"You get around, don't you? I mean, over and under ground both."

"True."

"In your travels have you happened to notice any single females?"

"There's a garter snake over by the bridge. But she's too skinny for me. Besides, marriage is a fatal mistake."

"I meant woodchucks."

"Oh." The snake coiled himself up and scratched his head with the end of his tail. "Single female woodchucks. I can think of at least a dozen."

"Any you could recommend?"

The snake made a face.

"No?"

"It's hard for me to judge, woodchuck. You're all so furry, and you eat so much. And those shrill whistles. Other animals call you whistle pigs, you know."

Fred, who never whistled, frowned. "Thanks anyway," he said stiffly.

The snake uncoiled himself and headed for the bolt hole. But just before leaving he looked back.

"There is one with a nice smile."

"She likes sugar beets, right?" Fred said, remembering the giantess.

"No, she never goes to that greenhouse. She hardly goes out at all. I believe she's in mourning for her mother."

"Do you know where she lives?" Fred asked. A woodchuck who skipped meals to mourn her mother sounded promising.

"Under the big stump."

Fred thanked the snake for the tip and offered him a snack for the road. "A snail, perhaps?"

But the snake just made another face and slithered away.

The Snake's Tip

The big stump was on the other side of the stream. Fred had crossed it in the fall, when the stream was low, but now that it was spring, the water level was quite high. Woodchucks can swim. Some even enjoy it. But not Fred. Nor did he like the idea of using the bridge. Cars and trucks were dangerous, and worse, they spewed exhaust fumes that soiled and stunk up your fur.

"Nobody could be worth getting all wet or dirty for," he decided.

The next time Fred went over to the stream to wash his supply of food, he was surprised to see a fir tree lying across the rushing torrent. "Beavers," he said to himself. But on closer inspection he saw that the trunk had been blasted, not gnawed, and he recalled the bone-shivering crack that had followed the thunderclap the day he'd been stuck in the tree.

"Lightning," he murmured.

It was as if this car-free bridge had fallen here specially

for him, and as he made his way across it, he wondered if the mourning woodchuck might somehow be his destiny. But when he got to the big stump, he hesitated. Though the entrance to her burrow was in plain sight, between two roots, he wasn't the sort of woodchuck to walk into a stranger's house unannounced. He waited and watched, half hidden by a clump of wild columbine.

In a few minutes a young raccoon ambled up to the burrow entrance and called in:

"Babette?"

Out skipped a female woodchuck—a ravishing creature with a brilliant coat and sparkling eyes.

"What's up?" she said.

"Want to play hide-and-seek?" the raccoon asked.

"Hide-and-seek. Um, I don't think so."

"Oh, come on."

"Sorry, I'm not in a hide-and-seek kind of mood. Maybe another time."

The woodchuck ducked back into her burrow, and the raccoon heaved a sigh and trudged away. He was hardly out of sight when a mink showed up, holding a pinecone behind his back.

"Babette?"

The woodchuck reappeared.

"Hi!" said the mink. "It's been three days!"

"Has it?" said Babette.

"Three days and two hours. Look what I found!" The mink revealed his pinecone. "Better than that stick, huh?"

"What stick?"

"The one we threw in the water and followed downstream. Don't tell me you've forgotten!"

"Oh, yeah, the stick."

"Go ahead." The mink presented her with the pinecone, and she stepped closer to the bank and threw it into the stream.

"Great toss!" cried the mink. "Let's go!"

"You go," Babette said. "Last time those prickers caught in my fur."

Fred sympathized about the prickers but wondered if this could really be the woodchuck the snake had mentioned, the one who hardly went out at all. Instead of chasing after the pinecone, she ambled down the bank and

checked her reflection in the water. The mink remained behind, a statue of devastation.

"Excuse me, mink," Fred said softly, coming out from behind the columbine. "Do you know this woodchuck well?"

"Babette?" The mink sighed. "Every time I close my eyes, I see her. But she barely knows I exist."

Babette started whistling a tune, and a dreamy expression crossed the mink's face. "Isn't it heavenly?" he murmured.

But they weren't the only ones to hear the whistling.

"Now who can that be?" the mink said, scowling at the head that had popped out of the water.

"How about a dip, Babette?" called the swimmer.

"Not today, muskrat," Babette called back. "But thanks anyway."

"My goodness, she certainly is popular," Fred remarked.

"Everybody's crazy about Babette," the mink said, none too cheerfully.

"Do you happen to know if she lost her mother recently?"

"I believe she did, yes."

With that, the disconsolate mink slouched off into the underbrush. It wasn't long before Babette climbed back up the bank.

"Hiya," she said, spotting Fred. "Seen the otter?"

"The otter?"

"I think I'm in a mud-sliding mood. How about you?"

There were few things Fred was less in the mood for than sliding in mud, but before he could reply, three little woodchucks came tumbling out of the burrow, two so young they didn't even have fur coats yet.

"Where you going, Mama?" said the biggest, tugging on Babette's tail.

"I may go mud-sliding," she said.

"Can we come?"

"Not today, Matt."

"You always say that!"

"You know, I have a great idea. Why don't you all take a nice, long nap?"

As the children started to whine, an astounded Fred slipped off toward the fallen fir. The frivolous woodchuck had children! There was nothing he disliked more than children. They were so messy and noisy.

"Hey, woodchuck!" Babette called after him. "If you see the otter, tell him Babs is looking for him, will you?"

Fred hustled on across the barky bridge without so much as a glance over his shoulder. To think he'd come here looking for a wife! Halfway home he spotted the snake sleeping on a flat rock in the sun, but he gave him a wide berth. Snakes are sensitive to the slightest vibrations, and Fred didn't want to wake him. What could you say to someone who gave such crummy tips?

A Nice Smile

The bad dream continued to spoil Fred's sleep. It even spilled over into the daytime. He would be chomping away on some clover, chewing thoroughly as always, when something soft and warm would touch his shoulder. But there was never a soul around.

One afternoon, while lounging on the sofa in his wonderfully insulated living room, he thought he heard a cracking sound, like thunder, and went to his doorway to see what it was. Everything looked peaceful: blue sky, not a breath of wind, the only creatures in sight a pair of doves cooing on a branch of the birch.

That night the mysterious cracking sound capped off his bad dream. It was so loud he lay there shaking, unable to doze off again for over an hour. When he finally did, he drifted straight back into the dream, and once more it ended with a fur-raising thunderclap.

After a week of this, which seemed more like a month, Fred was a total wreck. His tail began to drag behind him, leaving wormlike trails on his dirt floors. Except in winter he'd never been a napper—nap-taking seemed to him a sloppy sort of behavior—but now he found himself dozing off at odd times during the day.

He put up a valiant struggle. Even after a wretched night's sleep, he would get up and clean. But one morning, while sweeping dust balls and leaf bits out his doorway, he collapsed in a heap right in his entrance mound.

He had his usual dream: the soft, warm head leaning on his shoulder, then the nightmarish crack. But today a whole new torture was added—tumbling into ice water!

He woke sputtering. Good grief! He really was soaking wet. He was in the stream, right under the fallen fir!

"Great dive, woodchuck!"

It was Babette. She was perched on his side of the stream, where an otter was smoothing out a mud slide for her. Fred paddled to the far shore, pulled himself up, and violently shook himself dry.

"Now I'm sleepwalking," he muttered.

It was the only possible explanation. He must have sleepwalked all the way to the fir and then, startled by the crack, slipped off.

"What next?" he groaned.

As if in answer to his question, the twin baby wood-chucks came rolling and squealing down the bank. Fred backed away in horror. Of all children, babies were the noisiest and messiest. But he wasn't subjected to them for long. A female woodchuck came down the bank, scooped them up, and carried them away.

Curious in spite of himself, he climbed up the bank. She was sitting by the stump, cleaning the riverbank mud from the babies.

"Look at me, Aunt Phoebe!" cried the older child, who was hopping up and down atop the stump. "Look at me!"

"Be careful, Matt," she said. "It's a long way down."

Aunt Phoebe, thought Fred. This meant she was probably Babette's sister. She was younger than Babette, and not as ravishing, with mild gray eyes and a neat brown coat.

"How do you do?" he said.

She must not have noticed him earlier, for she gave a start.

"I should introduce myself," he said. "My name's Fred."

She merely nodded.

"I, uh, I met Babette," he went on awkwardly. "She's your sister?"

"Yes, but I'm afraid she's out. You might drop by later."

"Oh, I wasn't looking for her."

She gave him a knowing look. "Babette's not always great about keeping dates."

"No, really, I just . . ."

"You mustn't blame her. She's so much in demand she just forgets things."

"But we didn't have a date—honest."

"Well, if you say so," she said doubtfully, going back to cleaning the tiny twins.

"I understand you recently lost your mother," he said. "You have my deepest sympathies, Phoebe."

She looked up, surprised. "Thank you."

"Well, I'm sorry to disturb you. You clearly have your paws full."

"Aren't they wonderful?" Phoebe said, smiling proudly.

The smile lit up her whole face, and it hit Fred that Phoebe, not Babette, might be the snake's woodchuck "with a nice smile." It gave him an odd feeling, this smile of hers, a feeling he'd never had in the greenhouse. In fact, the smile affected him much the way Babette's whistling had the mink. So in spite of his poor opinion of children, and the fact that the one on the stump was singlehandedly making more noise than a flock of crows, he told Phoebe that all three looked like fine specimens.

"Are you stuck . . . er, do you have to take care of them all the time?" he asked.

"Babette usually stays home on Sundays, to recuperate from the week. I like to take a walk in the afternoon."

Fred cleared his throat. "Could I join you next Sunday by any chance? I could show you my burrow, if you like."

Seeing Phoebe glance away, he feared he'd been too forward. He really had no idea what woodchucks did on dates. He was just so proud of his burrow it had seemed the logical destination.

"Or we could go for a walk along the stream," he said.

"That sounds—"

"Ow!"

Matt had tumbled off the stump onto the ground. Phoebe rushed to his side.

"My leg!" the youngster screamed.

"I think you'll live, dear," she said. "Lean on me."

She led the little woodchuck toward the burrow, shepherding the twin babies ahead of her. But just before disappearing inside she looked over her shoulder, giving Fred one more dose of her radiant smile.

25

March 5

While waiting by the columbine for Phoebe to come back out, Fred concluded that he owed the snake a heartfelt thank you. Phoebe seemed a very different sort of woodchuck from her sister. Maybe not as breathtaking, but still lovely and neat as a pin—and sweet and modest and considerate, besides.

It was hot for spring, and the columbine didn't provide much shade. After an hour or so, Fred began to suffer from prickly heat. What could be keeping her? "I know I asked if I could join her next Sunday," he said. "But did she agree?"

He got itchier and itchier and was actually considering dousing himself in the stream when a porcupine came waddling up. "Spying on Babette, eh," the porcupine chuckled.

"What?" Fred said. "Not at all."

"And bees don't go buzz-buzz. No problem, woodchuck, there's room for two."

With that, the insulting beast crowded into the

columbine's shade and stuck Fred's ear with one of his quills. Fred stalked off in disgust and started across the fallen fir.

"Seen Babette?"

Now it was that otter, calling from the foot of his mud slide.

"I thought she was with you," Fred said.

"I was showing her how long I could stay under-water—and when I came up, she was gone!"

"Maybe she was afraid you were drowning and went for help."

"She probably just got bored and went off with some-body else. Females!"

The sleek creature slid into the water, and as Fred continued on his way, he echoed the otter's sentiment, muttering "Females!" under his breath. When you asked someone on a date, shouldn't they have the decency to give you a firm answer before you got prickly heat and poked by porcupines?

But once he was having his dinner in his nice, cool burrow, he forgave Phoebe completely. How could you expect a woodchuck to remember you were waiting when she had all those little monsters to deal with?

When he went out to forage for food the next day, the sky was overcast, and every time he glanced up, he thought of Phoebe's mild gray eyes. That evening, he sat in his favorite armchair by the glowworms, but instead of casting their usual spell of snug contentment, they just made him long for the glow of Phoebe's smile. In his dream that night, it was Phoebe who leaned her head on his shoulder, and there was no horrible cracking noise.

Unsure as he was about their date, he was soon counting the hours till Sunday afternoon. And unsure as he was that she would want to see his burrow even if they had a date, he spent Friday and Saturday doing a thorough spring cleaning. On Sunday morning he went all the way to the pig farm to pick some lilacs from the hedge in front of the farmhouse. After arranging the flowers in his living room, he went over to the stream, where he collected some duck feathers and picked a single forget-me-not. With the feathers, he gave the whole burrow a good dusting, after which he cleaned the bird droppings off the top of the entrance mound. Last of all, he cleaned and brushed himself.

As soon as he got across the fir tree, he spotted Phoebe sitting beside the stump all by herself.

"I was beginning to wonder if you'd forgotten," she said.

His heart swelled. She'd been expecting him!

"Since you're in mourning," he said, presenting her with the forget-me-not. "A possum once told me forget-me-nots are for remembrance."

"What a beautiful blue. Thank you, Fred."

"We're lucky with the weather, aren't we?"

"Mm."

"I guess your sister's inside with the br—the children?"

"Actually, she got antsy and took them on an outing."

"Which way?"

"Upstream."

"Maybe we should head downstream?"

"If you like. But it's awfully muddy along the bank."

"True," Fred said, impressed by her good sense.

"Would you care to see a favorite spot of mine?"

"By all means."

They walked across the fir tree and over a rutty field and started climbing a hill. When Phoebe stopped by a sparkling spring about halfway up, Fred was afraid she was going to suggest a swim, but she just put the forget-me-not by a stone at the water's edge. "My mother's grave," she said. "She liked being near water, but the stream rises and falls. The spring always stays the same."

"Quite a view from up here. Panoramic, you might say. See that birch tree over there? That's by my burrow."

"I love birches."

"Would you . . . care to see it?"

"Well, I've seen birch trees before."

"My burrow, I mean."

"Oh." Phoebe looked down at the forget-me-not on the grave. She loved her sister, and she adored Babette's kids, but even so, she'd been missing her mother terribly. Her mother had been steady and sensible, and often shared her opinions on things—sort of like this Fred, she thought, looking up at him.

"I couldn't stay too long."

Fred led her happily back down the hill and across the field. But he grew nervous as they neared his burrow. It was the first time he'd ever invited someone over.

"How beautiful!" Phoebe said when they stepped inside.

"You really think so?"

"Why, it's a showplace."

"I made the sofa. The chairs are inherited."

"They go wonderfully together. And such marvelous lighting!"

"They like it here," he said, smiling at his jarful of glow-worms. "They go out to feed now and then, but never all at once, and they always come back."

"Everything's so tidy. You wouldn't believe what our place is like, with the kids."

"I can imagine."

"I try, but it's a losing battle."

He showed her the kitchen.

"What a nice bowl, Fred."

"Thanks, I gnawed it myself. Soft pine."

"Lots of clover, I see."

"Mm, I've always been partial to it."

"Same here. I always say rabbits can have the grass."

"Rabbits," Fred said, rolling his eyes.

"Aren't they the stupidest things?"

"Totally brainless."

Back in the living room, she sat in a chair and sniffed the lilacs. "My favorite smell," she murmured.

"Mine, too!"

"You know how you wake up from hibernation feeling so groggy you just want to drop back to sleep?"

"Oh, yes."

"Well, I always think of lilacs blooming, and that helps me get up."

"When did you wake up this year?"

"I totally missed Groundhog Day. I didn't wake up until March fifth."

Fred gaped at her, astounded.

"Morning or evening?" he asked.

"Midday."

"But it's unbelievable! That's exactly when I woke up! Midday on March fifth."

"Goodness. What a coincidence."

It truly was. Fred was so struck by it that he had an urge to ask her then and there if his burrow was the sort of place she could imagine moving into. Indeed, most woodchucks would have. As a rule, woodchuck courtships take less than an hour.

But Fred wasn't most woodchucks.

"Would you care for a snail?" he asked.

A Rainbow

Later, when Fred returned from walking Phoebe home, his beloved burrow seemed so empty that he had half a mind to go back to the big stump. But the babies had been squalling when they got there and he knew she would be busy feeding them. She'd said she would be busy all week—till Sunday, their next date.

Fred's days had always been solitary, but that week, for the first time, they were lonely. Instead of eating his clover, he would just gaze at it, thinking how he and Phoebe both preferred it to grass. Outdoors, instead of foraging for food, he would stare at rabbits, thinking how he and Phoebe shared a low opinion of them, or stand downwind of lilac bushes, inhaling the fragrance they both liked. Instead of sleeping at night, he would lie there marveling at how they'd both woken up from their hibernation at the same time on the same day. When, toward the end of the week, a storm kicked up and blew a strip of birch bark down into his living room, he hung it on his bedroom wall instead of tossing it out, a tribute to Phoebe's love of birches.

On Saturday the storm system brought heavy rains, and though his burrow was as watertight as ever, Fred was miserable, afraid the rain might keep up and ruin their date. When he woke the next morning, he rushed to his doorway without even making his bed. Thank goodness! The clouds had vanished overnight. The sun was back, and the world looked newer and more radiant than he'd ever seen it.

He crossed the fir an hour earlier than last week, this time carrying a purple violet. To his inexpressible joy, he saw that Phoebe was early, too, already waiting outside her burrow.

"How lovely," she said, taking the flower.

"Not half as lovely as you," he said, surprising himself.

Phoebe was surprised, too. She was used to creatures

mooning over Babette's beauty, but not hers. And Fred was such a polite, respectable, good-looking woodchuck. "What a nice thing to say," she said. "But . . . have you lost weight?"

"I was a little off my food this week."

"You weren't sick, I hope."

"No, it's just . . . I missed you, Phoebe."

"You did?"

"Very much."

She studied the violet. The twins had had spring colds most of the week and she'd been run ragged taking care of them, but having today to look forward to had made it all a breeze. "I missed you, too, Fred," she said.

Just like that, Fred's absent appetite came rushing back. After leaving the violet on her mother's grave, they headed for his burrow and he fixed them Sunday dinner.

"I guess your digestion's improved," Phoebe remarked after he cleared the table.

Fred had finished off six snails and two bundles of clover. "I made a pig of myself," he said, embarrassed.

"A whistle pig," she said, smiling. "Don't you hate it when they call us that?"

"I can't stand it. Or groundhogs."

"I know. As if we all like to dig in the ground."

"Do you hate digging as much as I do?"

"I can't bear it. You can't get your paws clean for days."

"And don't you hate that stupid tongue twister about how much wood could a woodchuck chuck?"

"Gosh, yes, it's horrid. The only thing it's good for is

teaching babies to talk." She smiled. "Pretty soon I suppose I'll have to try it on the twins."

"They don't talk yet?"

"Good heavens, no—they're too young. Couldn't you tell?"

"I don't know very much about children."

"But you like them, don't you?"

"Frankly, no."

"I bet you just don't know any."

"Exactly how I'd like to keep it."

Fred's crusty tone made Phoebe smile. She'd heard about bachelors pretending to dislike kids—till they got married and had some of their own.

"Speaking of which," he went on, "don't you think it would be better for those kids if your sister played a bigger role in their upbringing? She *is* their mother."

"Well, you may be right, but it isn't likely to happen anytime soon. Babs enjoys getting out and about too much."

"It would happen if you weren't around."

"True. But as far as I know, I'm quite healthy."

"I didn't mean dying! I meant—if you didn't live there anymore."

"But it's my home."

Fred took a deep breath. By asking for her paw he would be sacrificing his blessed solitude, but Phoebe seemed so tidy, and soft-spoken, and so appreciative of his burrow. Surely she wouldn't disrupt his peace and quiet too much. And he couldn't remember a moment since meeting her when they hadn't been perfectly in tune—

unless it was when she got gooey about those kids. And even that wasn't really a mark against her. There was a considerable distance—and a stream—between his burrow and theirs. And besides, if she could be so patient with dirty, noisy brats who weren't even hers, he could only imagine how loving she would be to her own husband.

"You know, Phoebe," he said. "I was thinking you might come and live here."

"Here!"

They were sitting in his inherited chairs. Fred got out of his and knelt in front of her. "As my wife. Could you conceive of doing me such an honor?"

Phoebe wasn't caught completely off guard. Things had seemed to be heading in this direction. And though she did worry about the kids, about how well Babette would make out raising them on her own, she knew it was time for her to start a

life and family of her own. She and Fred seemed perfectly suited to each other, and this old-fashioned pro-
posal touched her deeply. Nothing could have been more
flattering than having a woodchuck with such neat and
formal habits kneel on the floor this way.

"Yes, I could conceive of it," she said, looking into his
eyes. "In fact, I think the honor would be mine."

Hearing this, Fred felt just the way the world had
looked that morning: fresh and new. He stood up and
dusted himself off. Phoebe stood as well and, smiling her
bright smile, opened her arms. But hugging mussed your
fur terribly, so Fred opted for sitting down on the sofa and
patting the place beside him.

After a confused moment, Phoebe sat, too.

"You've made me a very happy woodchuck, Phoebe."

So saying, Fred put an arm around her, just as the fat,
ugly human being he'd seen from the tree had put an arm
around his fat, ugly wife. And in a moment Phoebe leaned
her head on his shoulder, just as the fat woman had leaned
hers on her husband's shoulder.

Closing his eyes, Fred saw a rainbow.

Nine

Mr. and Mrs. Hubble, the fat, ugly human beings, lived in a town about a mile from Fred's burrow. They had nine children. The five oldest were fairly well behaved, but the last four were terrors—especially the youngest. When Mrs. Hubble got home from her job at the post office and saw the jam stains on the walls and her husband dozing in front of the TV, she would sigh and think, "If only we'd stopped at five."

Life had been sunnier back then. In those days, Mr. Hubble had been a carpenter and Mrs. Hubble had stayed home. But their appetites had gotten the better of them. For breakfast they had syrupy pancakes and bacon. For lunch, ham sandwiches plastered with mayonnaise, corn chips, and chocolate shakes. For dinner, pot roast with potatoes and gravy. For dessert, cupcakes or sundaes, and later, in front of the TV, popcorn slathered in melted butter. The sad day came when Mr. Hubble, the biggest eater of the bunch, could no longer climb ladders without breaking the rungs. He lost his job.

When their car was repossessed, Mrs. Hubble took her job sorting mail. Mr. Hubble stayed home and guzzled beer, only budging to go to the supermarket or his cousin's pig farm, where they got cut-rate hams. By this time there were eight children, and while they all had names, beer drinking made Mr. Hubble so fuzzy-headed he simply numbered them. He called the two youngest boys Six and Eight and the youngest girl Seven. Six, Seven, and Eight were very undisciplined. They never said "Please" and never passed the rolls and butter.

In the old days Mrs. Hubble had been merely chunky. Raising children was strenuous work. But all she did at the post office was sit, and though her waist size couldn't quite match Mr. Hubble's, she expanded considerably. One day she stepped on the scale she used to weigh large packages and was appalled to see she'd put on fifteen pounds. She cut out bacon and cupcakes, but a few weeks later she found she'd put on five more pounds. Her heart sank. There was only one possible explanation: she must be pregnant again.

Their ninth child was a little girl, and her name was Sally, but Mr. Hubble just called her Nine. By the time she was two years old, Nine put

Six, Seven, and Eight to shame in the bad-table-manners department. Leaning out of her high chair, she snatched

things right off her brothers' and sisters' plates. If they tried to take the food back, she howled—a howl so piercing they all had to cover their ears. As soon as they did, she would grab more. She ate so much that she usually tottered over if she tried to walk, so she preferred to crawl. As for talking, she could babble a few phrases, but she rarely did. Howling was more effective.

Nine made her brothers' and sisters' lives so miserable that one day Six and Seven and Eight, who had to share a room with her, called a secret meeting in their tree hut in the backyard.

"We've got to do something about the monster," said Six.

"Rat poison?" Eight suggested.

"We'd have to buy it," Six said. "They'd trace it to us."

"There's the axe," Seven said.

"Too messy," said Six.

But they finally hatched a plan.

One night early in June, after their mother dragged herself up to bed and their beery father dozed off in front of the TV, Six snuck down to the kitchen for a banana, peeled it, and met Seven and Eight back upstairs. The three of them tiptoed over to Nine's crib, shoved the whole banana into her mouth, and carted her out of the house.

They headed straight out of town and passed the last house before Nine managed to swallow the last of the banana and let out a "Whaaaa!" Down a country road they went, past a greenhouse glimmering in the moonlight. Before reaching the pig farm, they cut across a meadow, through some trees, and dumped their cargo in a ditch. Six, Seven, and Eight then skedaddled home.

Poor Nine was in shock. It was the first time she'd ever been dumped in a ditch in the dark. How could her brothers and sister do this to her? She howled at the top of her lungs, but for once her howling had no effect.

After a while she clambered out of the ditch and crawled along in her nightdress, shrieking every time a pebble or a pine needle jabbed one of her chubby knees. But eventually she looked up and saw the street lamp outside her bedroom window. In the bedroom was her crib, with its nice soft mattress, and her teddy bear. Best of all, two peanut-butter cookies she'd snatched were hidden under the pillow. She crawled faster, almost tasting the cookies. But the street lamp—it was actually the moon—never seemed to get closer. And since she wasn't used to all this fresh air and exercise, she finally collapsed at the foot of a tree and fell fast asleep.

Lousy Luck

The tree she collapsed under was the birch tree near Fred's burrow—or, rather, Fred and Phoebe's burrow, since they'd now been together several weeks. By woodchuck standards that made them an old married couple. Now two woodchucks woke up every morning at nine. Fred preferred twin beds—sleeping together mussed your fur—but he and Phoebe would wake up at the same instant, rub the sleep out of their eyes, look at each other, and smile. After a nice, civilized breakfast, they cleaned house. They spent most afternoons foraging for food, and later they fixed dinner together. In the evenings they reminisced about the day by the light of the glowworms till they started to yawn, then they padded off to bed.

One morning a dreadful wailing woke them two hours early.

"What a racket!" Phoebe exclaimed, sitting up in bed. "Do you suppose it's that brown bear we saw last week?"

"Sounds more like a moose," Fred said. "I believe it's their mating season."

They went to the entrance mound and stood there blinking till their eyes adjusted to the rays of the just-risen sun. The wailing went on, but there wasn't a moose in sight.

"You'd think they'd be too big to hide," Phoebe said. "Especially with those silly antlers."

"Let's go back to bed."

But in fact the noise was too shrill to sleep through, and when Phoebe headed for the birch tree—it seemed to be coming from thereabouts—Fred followed. Much as he hated getting morning dew on his fur, he hated the idea of her facing a moose alone even more.

It wasn't a moose. It was a plump human child. Fred instantly backed away from the deafening thing. Not because it looked dangerous but because it was so repulsive.

The creature's nightdress was filthy and covered with burrs, and its face and hands and feet were smeared with mud.

"Are you all right, child?" Phoebe said, going right up to it. "Where are your parents?"

Nine just wailed louder. What was this nasty, hairy-faced beast peering at her?

"We should be getting back, Phoebe," Fred shouted over the din.

"But, Fred! We can't leave the poor thing out here."

"Why not?"

"She's just a baby."

"She's awfully big for a baby."

"But she's lost."

"She seems to have found her way here. No doubt she can find her way back where she came from."

Phoebe tugged him aside. "You mustn't talk like that in front of her," she whispered.

"Why not? She can't understand us."

"How do you know?"

"Even if she could, she couldn't hear us over her own caterwauling. Besides, what on earth could we do for her?"

"Take her home."

"We don't know where she lives."

"To the burrow, I mean."

"Our burrow? You can't be serious, Phoebe."

"She's helpless."

"She certainly doesn't sound it. Besides, if we move her, the parents won't be able to find her."

After making this convincing point, Fred strode rather smugly back to the burrow. It was early for breakfast, but since the wailing ruled out going back to bed, he arranged

portions of clover on the table. However, Phoebe didn't join him. And he was so used to having all his meals with her now, so used to discussing the freshness of the food and their plans for the day, that he found he couldn't eat alone.

He went back to the entrance mound. To his horror, she was shoving the bawling child his way.

"Let her be, sweetheart! Come have breakfast!"

But Phoebe either couldn't or wouldn't hear him.

"Of all the lousy luck," Fred said, talking to himself for the first time in weeks.

Since becoming a couple, he and Phoebe had had only one argument. After returning from a visit to her sister and the kids, Phoebe had brought up the alarming idea of starting a family of their own, and when he'd made the obvious objection—that children turned life topsy-turvy— she'd replied without a shred of logic that topsy-turvy wasn't necessarily so terrible. Of course not even she could argue his point that she was very young and they hadn't even been together a season yet. But now this wretched human child had landed smack on their doorstep!

All by herself Phoebe managed to push the thing right up to the entrance mound.

"What in the world are you doing?" he said, astonished by her strength.

"If that bear comes back," Phoebe said, "he'll rip the poor thing to shreds."

"Well, she's certainly not coming in my burrow."

Phoebe gave Fred a long look. Much as she loved him, she longed for someone to hug and cuddle—things Fred never did.

"Then I'll just have to take her to Babette's," she said.

Fred watched, speechless, as Phoebe pushed the creature off in the direction of the stream. He hated it when she went to the big stump. Sometimes she stayed away for hours and he missed her terribly.

"When will you be back?"

"Hard to say," Phoebe called over her shoulder.

"You'll never get that thing across the fir tree!"

But again she either couldn't or wouldn't hear him. Her strength really was mind-boggling. In five minutes she and the bawling creature were nearly out of sight.

The Houseguest

Though the child was bawling away and covered with dirt, Phoebe found the feel of her very satisfying. Even so, she dreaded arriving at Babette's. Since she'd moved out, the burrow under the stump had grown more chaotic than ever, and the last thing it needed was added confusion. But while she was still on this side of the stream, Phoebe's progress was suddenly stopped.

She poked her head around the child to see whether they'd come up against a rock or a tree—and saw that they'd come up against Fred.

"Let's take the thing home," he said over the bawling.

If Phoebe hadn't known how he hated having his fur mussed, she would have thrown her arms around him. As it was, she smiled her warmest smile and said, "Thanks, sweetheart."

Working shoulder to shoulder, the woodchucks got the child back to the burrow in short order. They squeezed her in the entrance mound—Phoebe pulling, Fred pushing—and down into the living room.

"This is our home," Phoebe said brightly.

Nine looked around and wailed louder than ever. Now the hairy beasts had dragged her into a hole in the ground! But screaming at the top of her lungs took a lot of energy and she soon conked out on the floor.

The woodchucks slipped into the kitchen so they could talk without disturbing her. They both spoke at once.

"We should get her some food," said Phoebe.

"We should get her cleaned up," said Fred.

Since Fred had just given in to her, Phoebe gave in to him this time. He went for moss; she filled the bowl from the stream. Back in the burrow they gently pulled off the child's dirty nightdress and delicately sponged her with damp moss, careful not to wake her. Then Phoebe washed the nightdress in the stream while Fred went out to collect food. He brought back two bundles of fresh clover, some tasty-looking greens, an assort-ment of insects, and three nice, juicy snails.

When the child woke up, late that afternoon, she looked around the burrow in horror and disgust. Why was she lying naked in this hole? Where were her crib and peanut-butter cookies? Two

bristly, beady-eyed faces were peering at her—the beasts who'd dragged her underground.

"Don't worry, you're safe with us," Phoebe said. "Do you have a name?"

Nine just blubbered.

"I guess she's too young to know," Phoebe said.

"Or too dumb."

"Don't say that!" Phoebe said. "What shall we call her?"

"Why call her anything?" said Fred, who trusted their guest's stay would be brief.

"Everyone has to have a name. What do you think of Margaret?"

"Why Margaret?"

"It was my mother's name," said Phoebe, who'd always intended to name her first child that.

Fred shrugged.

"We got you some nice clover, Margaret," Phoebe said, holding out a bunch.

The child knocked it away and blubbered louder. Phoebe handed her a clump of greens. The child turned her nose up at that, too. Where were her mashed potatoes and gravy? Where was her hot fudge sundae? Before she knew it, the horrid creatures were holding out bugs and snails!

"Maybe she's more thirsty than hungry," Phoebe said. "Would you get some fresh water, dear?"

Fred wasn't sorry to escape Margaret's shrieks and the

mess she'd made of the living room: greens and clover
and snails scattered everywhere.

Ten minutes later he returned from the stream with
the refilled bowl. The child took a sip of the water and
spat it out in his face.

"Yuck!"

"Oh, dear," said Phoebe, drying Fred off.

"Clearly she doesn't want our help," Fred said coldly.
"I think the sooner she's out of here the—"

"Hush!" Phoebe said. "She'll understand you."

And in fact Margaret was catching on to the animals'
way of speaking. One of the good things about being very
young is that your brain's so uncluttered it's easy for new
things to fit in.

"Hungry!" Margaret cried, attempting animal talk.

"I really think she wants something to eat," Phoebe said. "We'll just have to figure out what she likes."

By this time there wasn't much daylight left. Fred and Phoebe scurried around in the twilight, gathering up every kind of grass and weed available. But when they offered these delicacies to their houseguest, she threw them on the floor or spat them back in their faces. Normally, at this hour of the day, she would have been perched in her high chair, stuffing her face with pot roast and buttered bread and grabbing assorted goodies off her brothers' and sisters' plates. But here she was, stuck in a hole with a pair of stubbly beasts who kept trying to force-feed her things that weren't even food.

On top of that, they seemed to expect her to sleep in a bed half the size of her crib. While the smaller beast lay down on the other bed, the bigger one went out to the living room and put out the light. Instead of blubbering, Nine lay silently in the darkness, waiting for her kidnappers to doze off. Having snoozed all day, she wasn't the least bit sleepy.

After quite a long time she groped her way out of the bedroom. A leaf was draped over the jar of funny lit-up worms, but a bit of the weird greenish glow leaked through, and as she crawled past the sofa, where the bigger beast was lying, she caught the glimmer of two open eyes. To her surprise, he didn't try to block her escape.

The nightdress they'd stolen from her was hanging in

the breezy entranceway. It was still a little damp, but she did her best to put it on. Outside, a white tree stood out against a black sky. She started toward it, led on by visions of peanut-butter cookies, but after crawling a few feet she heard a growl and turned to see her teddy bear—except twenty times bigger, with knifelike teeth that glinted menacingly in the moonlight.

Milk and Honey

A second after the scream, Phoebe stumbled out of the bedroom, rubbing her eyes. "What on earth was that?"

Fred sat up on the sofa with a sinking heart. He'd hoped he'd heard and seen the last of the child when it crawled past him.

"I'm not sure," he lied.

"Where's Margaret?"

"Um, isn't she in bed?"

"No, she's—"

Another scream—and off Phoebe dashed.

Soon she was pushing the child back down into the living room. "Poor Margaret, she's scared out of her wits," Phoebe said. "That bear was marauding around out there."

Fred couldn't help thinking Margaret's shrieks would have been less piercing if she'd been tucked safely away in the bear's stomach, but of course he kept this to himself. And though he got precious little sleep that night, he accompanied Phoebe food-hunting in the morning. This time they tried flowers. It was getting summery, and there were plenty to pick: buttercups, daisies, dandelions, red clover. When they got back to the burrow, Margaret grabbed the pretty bouquet and stuffed it greedily into her mouth.

"Ick!" she cried, spitting it out.

Though Phoebe didn't seem to mind getting sprayed with dandelion juice, Fred certainly did. Halfway to the stream he tripped over a stick.

"Why don't you watch where you're going!"

"Sorry," said Fred, realizing the stick was actually the striped snake.

"You know, woodchuck, you don't look so hot," the snake said. "You look run-down, and your fur . . ."

"I know, I know."

"Wife on the warpath, I suppose. Didn't I tell you marriage is a fool's game?"

"It's not Phoebe. It's this child she's taken in."

"Orphaned woodchuck?"

"Human. It's a nightmare, snake. The monster won't eat a thing, so all she does is bawl."

The snake coiled himself up and scratched his head with the tip of his tail. "Human, eh. Want my advice?"

"Certainly."

"Boot it out."

"I couldn't agree more. But Phoebe . . ."

"I see," the snake said, giving him a pitying look. "Well, I know some folks who might be able to help you."

"Who?"

"There's a squirrel—one of my roommates, actually. He could show you where to find nuts. Then there's that wild goat who mows the meadow. If you caught her on a good day, she might give you some of her milk. Then there's this bear who's been hanging around."

"You talk to bears?"

"Of course not," the snake said impatiently. "But if you follow him, he might lead you to honey. And you could check with one of these flighty birds about where the ripest berries are."

It was Fred's turn to scratch his head. He'd never have thought of inedible things like nuts or milk or honey or berries. But then, the snake had steered him to Phoebe.

"Thanks, snake."

"One more piece of advice."

"Yes?"

"Get some sleep and clean yourself up." And with that, the snake slid off through the grass.

Fred did give himself a thorough scrubbing on the bank of the stream. But as for a desperately needed nap, he got back to the burrow to find Margaret bawling away, ignoring Phoebe's attempts to comfort her. Fred, who wouldn't have minded a little comforting himself, tugged Phoebe into the kitchen.

"This can't go on," he said.

"I know. The poor child's starving."

That wasn't what he'd meant at all. But since it was clear that Phoebe wasn't ready to give up on the dreadful creature quite yet, he told her what the snake had advised.

"Nuts and berries?" she said doubtfully. "Milk and honey?"

"I know it sounds crazy, but I suppose we could give it a try. Anything to shut her up."

"All babies cry."

"Why don't you find the goat, and maybe a bird. I'll look for the squirrel and the bear."

"Be careful of that bear, dear," Phoebe said, squeezing his paw.

Fred found the snake sunning himself on his flat rock by the edge of the meadow. "Excuse me for disturbing you again, snake, but have you seen that squirrel you mentioned?"

The snake let out a startlingly loud hiss. Soon a squirrel came scampering up.

"You called?" the squirrel said.

"Squirrel, woodchuck," said the snake. "Woodchuck, squirrel."

"It's a pleasure to meet you," the squirrel said.

"Likewise," Fred said, trying to sound sociable.

"Wants some nuts," the snake explained.

"Really?" said the squirrel. "I never knew woodchucks cared for nuts."

"Not for me," Fred said. "It's a long story."

"Oh, I love stories," the squirrel said.

"He doesn't want to tell stories," the snake snapped, "he wants nuts."

"Of course, sorry," said the squirrel. "Just follow me, woodchuck."

The squirrel led Fred into some woods and generously revealed where he'd hidden supplies of chestnuts and acorns and hazelnuts. After stuffing a sampling into his cheeks, Fred thanked the squirrel in a garbled voice and trotted home. Phoebe wasn't back yet; in their absence Margaret had splintered one of his inherited chairs.

Spitting out the nuts, Fred tried to swallow his rage. "Have one of these," he said, handing the miserable child a chestnut.

"Yicky!" she said, hurling it.

The nut ricocheted off the wall and hit Fred in the thigh.

"Well, try one of these," he said, giving her an acorn.

Margaret had a remarkable arm, and when he got the

acorn back in the gut, he doubled over in pain. A few inches from his face was one of her bare feet. Woodchuck teeth are like razors, and it would have been deeply satisfying to nip one of the ogre's toes. But her feet were so filthy he was afraid of germs.

Just as Fred straightened up, Phoebe came in, carrying the bowl. "What a marvelous goat!" she said. "We had a real mother-to-mother talk—and look!"

The bowl was half full of goat's milk.

"Duck when you give it to her," Fred advised, backing away.

But Margaret didn't spit the milk out. In fact, after sticking her tongue into the bowl for a taste, she slurped it all up.

"She likes it!" Phoebe said triumphantly. "Isn't it wonderful?"

The milk had left a hideous mustache on Margaret's face. "Wonderful," Fred mumbled.

"Hungry!" Margaret squawked.

"She didn't like the nuts?" Phoebe said, noting the ones on the floor.

"Not exactly."

"We better go back out."

While Phoebe went in search of a bird, Fred plodded over the rutty field and up the hill to the spring. From there you could see most of the countryside; but, unhappily, he didn't spot a single human being out searching for a lost child. However, he did make out a fuzzy brown shape lumbering along the edge of the woods he'd just visited with the squirrel.

Fred tromped wearily down the hill and headed that way, keeping a healthy distance between himself and the bear. Before long, the beast stood on his hind legs and stuck his head into a hole in a tree. He was quickly surrounded by a nasty swarm of bees, but even so it was quite a while before he pulled his head out and went back down on all fours. He ambled away, smacking his lips.

Fred approached the bee tree gingerly. It was a half-dead pine with deeply grooved bark, ideal for climbing. He scrabbled up and peered in at a hollowed-out trunk lined with comb upon comb of honey. The bees crawling on them didn't take him very seriously. In fact, several laughed at the sight of him. Still, when he leaned in and pried off a comb, one bee was annoyed enough to sting him right on the tenderest part of his snout.

Though not heavy, the comb was horribly gooey and

gave off a revoltingly sweet
smell. By the time Fred had
lugged it back to the burrow, he felt nauseous.

Phoebe, who'd beaten
him home, was all
smiles.

"Margaret adores
the berries," she cooed.

It certainly looked
that way. Margaret now
had a purple-smeared
chin to go with her milk
mustache.

"I got a terrible bite
on my—"

Before Fred could fin-
ish his sentence, Margaret
snatched the honeycomb
out of his paws. She de-
voured it whole.

"I told you everything would work out!" Phoebe cried,
clapping for joy. "Isn't it fantastic?"

Fred said nothing. He was busy licking the horrid
honey off his front paws so he could try to work the
stinger out of his snout.

The Cave

A few weeks later the striped snake was sunning himself on his favorite rock when he heard a rustling in the grass. He didn't so much as twitch; only his yellowish-green eyes shifted. Several yards away a female field mouse was making her way along, sniffing at this and that. It wasn't till she was just a couple of snake-lengths from the rock that she sensed danger and looked up.

The snake struck. Unluckily—for him, at least—he had to negotiate a clump of tall grass and just missed the mouse's tail, losing the advantage of surprise. But he was hungry and dashed after her anyway. The mouse darted left, then right, then dove into a hole.

It was the bolt hole of a woodchuck's burrow. The field mouse sprinted through the living room without so much as a "Pardon me," but the snake stopped in confusion, letting the mouse escape out the front entrance. He could have sworn this was the burrow of his woodchuck acquaintance. But that was always neat as could be. The

floor here was stained with rancid milk and berry juice, and the walls were all gooey, with splintered wood and broken nutshells stuck to them.

"Where am I?" he wondered aloud.

"Shhhh," said a woodchuck, trudging out of the kitchen.

The woodchuck was so worn and exhausted it took the snake a moment to recognize him. "What's going on around here?"

"Don't wake her," Fred said, pointing at the bedroom.

The snake peered into the bedroom. It was entirely filled by a softly snoring creature with neither fur nor scales.

"Ah, the human. I see you tried some of the food I mentioned."

Fred moaned. "All she does is eat. She's twice the size she was."

"What happened to your furniture?"

"Broken. Every piece of it."

"You look kind of broken yourself, woodchuck. Have you been eating enough?"

Fred glanced wistfully at the kitchen. "I try. But I don't seem to have any appetite."

"Maybe it's the smell."

"Charming, isn't it."

"Where's the wife?"

"Out getting goat's milk."

"Keep feeding the creature and you won't be able to get her out of the bedroom."

"I know, I know."

"Didn't I tell you to get rid of her?"

"Yes. But Phoebe loves the brute."

The snake decided against asking if the woodchuck's wife had a screw loose, and since he had nothing else to say, he slipped away. Being cold-blooded and selfish by nature, he was mainly annoyed at losing the mouse, but once he was coiled up on his favorite sunning rock again, he couldn't help feeling a bit sorry for the foolish woodchuck. To get married—and then, on top of that, to take in a human being!

A few days later, while hunting on the edge of the woods, the snake crossed paths with the squirrel. The squirrel started jabbering away as usual, but the snake simply tuned him out, as was his habit. They lived in the same cave, along with a skunk and a pair of bats.

After a while the squirrel gave the snake a nudge. "Isn't that your friend?" he said.

The snake looked around and saw the woodchuck stumbling toward them with a honeycomb in his paws and two bee bites on his snout. "Acquaintance," he said.

"He looks awful."

Squirrels are warm-blooded and have softer hearts than snakes, and when Fred got closer, the squirrel volunteered to carry the honeycomb. Fred blinked blearily. He was so drained he'd virtually been sleepwalking again and hadn't even noticed the two animals. If they'd been foxes, he would have been dinner.

"No use two of us getting all sticky, squirrel," Fred said. "But I appreciate the offer."

"Still getting squeezed out of house and home?" the snake asked.

Fred nodded despondently.

"We could put you up," the squirrel said. "We have tons of room."

"I couldn't possibly impose," Fred said. "But it's kind of you to offer."

"You haven't even seen the cave," the squirrel said, relieving Fred of the honeycomb. "Come on. What can you lose by looking?"

Fred, who didn't have the energy to protest, traipsed along after the squirrel. The snake trailed after them to protect his interests, not at all sure he liked the idea of more roommates. But he needn't have worried about Fred, who took a few steps into the cave and immediately started edging back out. It was big, but damp and messy, and there was a skunk in residence. As if a squirrel and a snake weren't enough!

"Skunk, this is a friend of snake's," said the squirrel.

"Good afternoon," the skunk said, swishing her impressive tail. "Are you from these parts?"

"More or less," Fred said. The cave was on the far side of the hill where Phoebe's mother was buried.

"Remarkable we've never run into each other."

"The truth is, I didn't used to cover much territory. Though nowadays . . ."

"He's being squeezed out of his home," said the squirrel. "Don't you think he should move in with us?"

"It's not just him," the snake hissed.

"You have a family, woodchuck?" the skunk asked.

"There's my wife and me," Fred said. "And, at the moment, a human child."

"Human?"

Fred nodded grimly.

"Remarkable!" said the skunk.

"That's one word for it."

"We never see human beings over this way."

"Well, they're not much to look at."

"Is that so?" squeaked a voice overhead. "We've flown over them, but we can't really see."

Fred stared up at a pair of wrinkly black creatures who were hanging upside down from the cave's ceiling.

"Sorry to wake you, bats," said the squirrel. "We have a guest."

71

As soon as Fred had been introduced to Mr. and Ms. Bat, he took the honeycomb off the squirrel's paws. "Thanks so much for having me over," he said, anxious to escape this zoo. "But I'm afraid I'm due home."

"You just got here!" the squirrel protested. "Don't you like it?"

"Do stay," said the skunk.

"Would you like us to fly out and get you a snack?" asked one of the bats.

"You're too kind," Fred said. "But I really do have to get this thing home."

The honeycomb prevented him from shaking paws, so he simply bid the cave dwellers good-bye. As he tottered away, he heard the friendly squirrel sigh—but a second later he was pretty sure he heard a hiss of relief escape the snake.

Mud

T hank heavens!" Phoebe said when Fred finally got home. "I was afraid you'd been stung to death!"

"Well, I—"

"Whaaa!" wailed Margaret, poking her head out of the bedroom.

"The poor thing's famished," Phoebe said.

The poor thing grabbed the honeycomb out of Fred's paws and wolfed it down.

"You did get a few stings, didn't you, sweetheart?" Phoebe said. "Are they bad?"

"Well, they're not good."

"But it's worth it to see her eat like this, isn't it?"

Fred just poked the bumps on his snout.

"Did you stop for a nap?"

"I wish. I got dragged off to a cave."

"A cave?"

"Where that striped snake lives. And the squirrel. Over on the far side of the hill with the spring."

"What's it like?"

"It's a dreadful place. Sort of a rooming house for ani-mals. Bats even."

"Is it spacious?"

"I suppose."

"You know, if we have to live somewhere else, Mother's hill would be a nice place. Her spirit could watch over us."

"I need some clover," Fred mumbled, heading for the kitchen.

He refused to discuss the cave further, even after another week of fetching honeycombs and sleeping on the living-room floor. But before long the human eating machine outgrew the bedroom, and though Fred was glad to get his bed back, life with Margaret occupying the

entire living room was grimmer than ever. It was dimmer, too. Whenever Margaret saw a glowworm slip out of the jar to find some food, she would try to catch it, and if she did she pulled it apart. Soon the few remaining glowworms were so scared and starved they barely glowed at all.

For Fred and Phoebe, sleeping till nine was no more than a rosy memory. Now they woke before seven, knowing Margaret would be yelling for food any second.

"I think the time's come for desperate measures, sweetheart," Phoebe said early one morning, smiling at Fred from her bed.

"What sort of desperate measures?" Fred asked groggily.

"Adding on."

"Adding on?"

"A new room. Now don't worry. I know you hate digging even more than I do. I'm going to do it myself, as soon as I get back from the goat."

Fred yawned and rolled over. But in fact he was wide-awake, and as soon as he heard Phoebe get the bowl and leave the burrow, he jumped out of bed and pulled the pictures off the far bedroom wall. Phoebe was right: the time had come for desperate measures. And she was right, too, about his despising digging more than anything. But she was wrong if she thought he was going to let her do it.

When Phoebe came home with a bowl of goat's milk, Margaret usually greeted her with a hungry whine. But this morning the child was giggling.

"What's so funny, dear?" Phoebe said, pleased to see her enjoying herself.

"Fred," said Margaret, who by now had mastered a fair amount of animal language.

"What about him?"

"All gone."

"He went to get you some nice honey?"

Margaret shook her head, smiling at the bedroom.

"You mean he's still in bed?" Phoebe said, dropping her voice to a whisper. "Good girl not to cry. He needs the sleep."

After handing Margaret the bowl, Phoebe went to peek at her late-sleeping husband and almost fainted. The bedroom was completely full of mud.

"What on earth?" she cried. "Where's Fred?"

"All gone," Margaret said, giggling some more.

Phoebe dug in a panic. When she unearthed Fred's tail, her heart stopped beating for several seconds, then she burrowed even more frantically.

Finally she was able to pull Fred out into a corner of the living room. He was caked with mud but, mercifully, still breathing.

"Fred? Fred?"

His eyes opened.

"Are you all right?" Phoebe cried, cradling his filthy head in her lap. "Say something!"

His eyes seemed to bulge. Instinctively, she sat him up and smacked him on the back. He coughed up a wad of mud.

"Thanks," he croaked.

"You poor dear! What happened?"

"I tried—" He coughed up another mud morsel. "I was trying to add on, then—a cave-in."

"How horrible," she said, picking mud out of his ears. "Are any bones broken?"

"I don't think so," Fred said, sitting up straighter.

But he was very feeble, and when he saw his mud-coated fur, and the mud-filled bedroom, he passed out.

"Margaret," Phoebe cried. "Help me get him into the fresh air!"

Margaret looked up from the bowl, milk drooling down her chin, and shook her head. "Too dirty," she said.

So Phoebe had to drag Fred outside by herself.

Moving Day

Instead of enlarging the burrow, Fred had managed to make it smaller. With no bedroom and Margaret hogging the living room, the only place left for the woodchucks to sleep was the kitchen.

One night of this was enough for Phoebe. "I really think we'd better try that cave," she said the next morning.

There was a time when nothing could have enticed Fred away from his beloved burrow. But that was before he'd been squirted with dandelion juice, pelted with nuts, stung by bees, coated with honey, and buried alive in mud—before his beloved burrow had been converted into a dark, sticky, smelly pit of honey, berry mush, and mud.

Margaret hadn't budged from the burrow since the night she'd seen the giant teddy bear with the big teeth, and she screamed as violently on being pushed out as she had the first time she was pushed in. She'd gotten used to it in there. She liked lolling around and being waited on hand and foot.

"We're going to a nice new place, sweetie," Phoebe

assured her, setting the bowl on Fred's head like a big cap. "It'll be an adventure."

Margaret didn't like the sound of "adventure." She didn't like exercise either, especially now that her weight had doubled. She walked for a little while, then got tired and crawled alongside the woodchucks, whining as she went. She finally plunked down on her tummy in the shade of a quaking aspen and fell fast asleep. Try as they might, the woodchucks couldn't wake her, so in the end they had no choice but to carry her. By the time they

dumped her at the mouth of the cave, Fred couldn't have gone another step.

"Hi, there!" said the squirrel, popping out.

"Hello," Fred said, panting.

"So this must be your wife."

"Phoebe," Phoebe said.

"Nice to meet you, Phoebe," said the squirrel. "Look, everybody, the human child!"

"Remarkable," the skunk said, stepping out. "What's its name?"

"Margaret," Phoebe said proudly.

"It looks very well fed," the skunk remarked.

"Doesn't she?" Phoebe said.

"Have you come to stay?" the squirrel asked hopefully.

"Well, if there's room, and you don't mind," Phoebe said, "we thought we might give it a try."

"Fine with us," said the skunk.

"Where's the snake?" Fred asked.

"Out hunting, probably," said the squirrel. "But I'm sure he'll be delighted."

Fred wasn't so sure about that, and after helping Phoebe get Margaret into the cave, he stationed himself outside to await the snake's return. Inside, the squirrel made such a to-do that the bats woke up and started flying in crazy circles around the cave. Phoebe was enthralled. Not just by the warm reception, but by the rock walls—no more cave-ins—and all the room there was for Margaret to grow in.

"Does she like nuts?" the squirrel asked. "I've got scads hidden."

"She didn't when Fred tried them on her," Phoebe said.

"Did he shell them?"

"Is that what you do?"

After retrieving a nut from a hiding place in the back of the cave, the squirrel removed the shell with his magnificent front teeth and presented the inner kernel to Margaret. She made a face, touched the nut with her tongue, then stuck it in her mouth. She chewed and swallowed.

"More!"

"She liked it!" the squirrel said joyfully.

"I wonder if she'd care to try some of my bugs?" the skunk said. "I have a couple of fresh crickets."

"That's a very kind offer," Phoebe said, "but I wouldn't risk it."

"What's her favorite food?" asked Mr. Bat, parking upside down on the ceiling again.

"Raspberries!" Margaret cried, answering for herself.

"Staggering," said the skunk. "She even speaks our language."

Mr. Bat whizzed out of the cave and quickly returned with a ripe raspberry, which he dropped into Margaret's hand like an expert bombardier. Margaret shoved it into her mouth.

"Thank the nice bat, dear," Phoebe said.

"More!" Margaret cried.

At dusk Fred spotted the snake. But instead of slithering in his usual way, he approached the cave like someone lugging heavy baggage. And, indeed, he was.

"Are you all right, snake?" Fred asked, gaping at the huge swelling in the middle of his slender body.

The snake gave him a drowsy smile. "Never better," he said. "You?"

"Well, er, I'm a little worried. You see, we had some problems at home, and we were thinking of moving in with you for a while—if you think you could stand it."

"Fine, fine," the snake said, smiling away.

The snake dragged himself into the cave, followed by a rather surprised woodchuck.

"Excuse me, squirrel," Fred said. "But what's with the snake?"

After giving Margaret another shelled nut, the squirrel looked around and saw the snake curling up in his sleeping place.

"Looks like a bullfrog," he said.

"A bullfrog?"

"His favorite food."

While the snake fell into a contented, digestive sleep, everyone else fussed over Margaret. Mr. and Ms. Bat flew out for berry after berry, the squirrel shelled nut after nut, and the skunk helped Fred and Phoebe collect leaves to make Margaret a comfortable bed.

Once she'd stuffed herself, Margaret plopped into her new bed.

"We won't make a peep," the squirrel promised. "Sweet dreams, Margaret."

Margaret grunted, then started snoring. Phoebe whispered her gratitude to the animals and, following Fred into a secluded nook of the cave, curled up next to him for the night—as close as she could get without mussing his fur.

Cave Life

Fred was back in his old burrow, sweeping. There wasn't a trace of mud anywhere. Everything was just so, as neat and tidy as when he and Phoebe first got married. And there was Phoebe, dusting with a cattail . . .

Margaret's snoring burst the delicate bubble of the dream. Blinking, Fred saw bats hanging upside down overhead, smelled the musky odor of skunk. He shut his eyes tight, trying to float back into the dream world. But morning light was already seeping into the cave, and before long Margaret was yelling:

"Food!"

Fred dragged himself out of the cave and shuffled off around the base of the hill. When he neared the bee tree, he saw that he would have to wait his turn. The bear was feasting today. So it was a good while before he got back to the cave, honeycomb in his paws, sting on his snout.

"Here you go, Margaret," he said, holding out the gummy thing.

But for a change Margaret didn't snatch it. "Full," she said.

"Isn't it a miracle, sweetheart?" Phoebe whispered. "Everybody pitches in."

It seemed the bats and the squirrel had already supplied Margaret with a sumptuous breakfast of berries and nuts. Fred set the honeycomb on a shelf of stone for Margaret's lunch.

While he went off to the stream to clean his paws, Margaret hunkered down for her after-breakfast nap. She was glad they'd moved to this cave. When it had gotten chilly in the middle of the night, she'd just shouted, "More leaves!" and the bats, who didn't seem to mind the dark, had flown out and fetched her some. Now she had more than just two woodchucks to boss around: she had a pair of bats as well, and a squirrel, and a skunk.

Margaret spent her days eating and napping, never budging from the cave, and the animals fell into a routine that revolved around her wants. Only one creature refused to wait on her.

"Nasty snake," Margaret said one morning. "No arms or legs."

"Shh," said Phoebe. "You'll hurt his feelings."

"He won't get berries!"

"Oh, are you hungry? Why didn't you say so, dear?"

Even though it was raining, Phoebe went out to find the child some berries.

It rained for several days in a row. One soggy afternoon

the squirrel came back to the cave soaked to the bone.

"You look like a rat," the snake remarked as the squirrel emptied his cheeks of nuts.

"Do I?" the squirrel said cheerfully. "Guess what I saw on the other side of the hill."

"What?"

"A bunch of woodchucks wandering around in the rain."

"What did they look like?" Phoebe asked.

"A grown-up female and three kids—two still pretty small."

"Oh, Fred, it sounds like Babette. We better go see what's wrong."

"If it's Babette, I'm sure it's just a lark," said Fred, who had no intention of getting drenched.

But when Phoebe rushed out, he naturally followed.

They found the four woodchucks huddled under a holly bush. It took a moment to recognize Babette. She wasn't her usual glamorous self at all.

"Phoebe, thank goodness!" said the bedraggled woodchuck. "I went by your burrow and found a horrid old badger squatting there."

While Phoebe hugged the moist children, Fred stared numbly at the driving rain. Now, on top of everything else,

his once lovely home had been taken over by a badger.

"I've been meaning to drop by to tell you we moved," Phoebe said, "but I've had my paws full. What are you doing out in this weather?"

"We woke up all wet, Aunt Phoebe!" Matt chirped. "It was cool!"

"The stream rose and flooded us out," Babette moaned. "We're homeless!"

"Don't be silly," Phoebe said, scooping up the two little ones. "Just follow us."

Oh, lord, thought Fred.

When they arrived back at the cave, the snake hissed out a laugh. "You look like a herd of possums," he said.

While Fred indignantly shook himself dry, Margaret scowled at the newcomers. "Who?" she said, pointing.

"It's not nice to point, dear," Phoebe said. "This is my sister, Babette, and these are her children—your cousins."

"No!"

"Well, not by blood, of course. But in a way Fred and I are your parents, and these are my niece and nephews."

"No room!" Margaret declared.

"No room, dear? What do you mean?"

"No room!"

For once, Fred agreed with the child.

"You mustn't say that, Margaret," Phoebe said. "Would the rest of you mind if they stayed for a while? Their burrow got flooded."

Except for the snake, who said nothing, the animals were all very cordial. The three little ones were exhausted and went right to sleep in a corner of the cave.

Babette took this opportunity to fix her fur. "Hiya," she said, noticing the coiled-up snake.

The snake grunted.

"What are you doing?" Babette asked.

"Trying to relax."

The snake coiled himself up the other way, so his head faced away from her—leaving Babette totally bewildered. In her whole life no one had ever reacted to her like this.

She was still in a state of confusion when the children woke from their naps and started running wild around the cave. The squirrel was out, the skunk had kindly gone with Phoebe to help carry back the bowl of goat's milk, and the bats were trying to doze, so it fell to poor Fred to try to get the brats under control.

Margaret, of all creatures, rescued him from his baby-sitting. She lunged at one of the smaller woodchucks, and when the tiny thing curled up in self-defense, she picked it up and bounced it off the wall like a furry little handball.

"Fun!" she cried.

She used all three of the youngsters for her game. They didn't seem to enjoy it as much as she did. One by one, they stumbled back to their corner and fell in a dazed heap. Fred almost felt like thanking the child.

The handball game was the most activity Margaret had

had since the move to the cave, and that evening she passed out early. The handballs themselves were pretty worn out, too. While Phoebe and the skunk helped Babette put them to bed, the squirrel laid out a cold buffet supper for the rest of them.

Babette was so fascinated by the snake she hardly touched a bite. "Have you always lived around here?" she asked, toying with her clover.

The snake, who'd just swallowed a partridge egg, couldn't have answered even if he'd wanted to.

"I think he told me he was born in the compost heap on the pig farm," the squirrel said, answering for him.

"Really?" said Babette. "How interesting!"

"Are you woodchucks all from around here?" the skunk asked.

"Fred's family goes back generations in this area," Phoebe said. "Doesn't it, dear?"

"We were here before the greenhouse went up," Fred said rather proudly.

"Remarkable," said the skunk. "I don't even know who my grandparents were."

"I hardly even knew my mother," the squirrel said.

"Why not?" Phoebe asked.

"She took off with a flying squirrel right after I was born."

"Good gracious."

The snake swallowed impatiently, getting the egg far enough down his gullet so he could speak. "That's nothing," he said hoarsely. "My mother got carried off by a chicken hawk and lived to tell the tale."

"How'd she escape?" Babette asked, wide-eyed.

"Nipped the silly bird on the leg and it dropped her. Landed smack in a cow pat. Smelly, but soft."

"Is she still alive?" Phoebe asked.

"Who knows?" said the snake with a shoulderless shrug. "I don't keep up with family much."

"Phoebe was saying her mother's buried right up the hill," the skunk said. "By a spring."

"I bet that's where we catch mosquitoes," Ms. Bat squeaked from above.

The creatures talked late into the night, till everyone but the bats started to yawn. When Fred and Phoebe crawled into their nook, she whispered, "It's friendly here, isn't it, dear?"

Fred, of course, would have much preferred to be back in their burrow—at least as it had been in the pre-Margaret days. But the darkness hid the cave's messiness, and just now, with Margaret dead to the world, he was willing to admit that things could have been worse.

Fun

When everyone was in bed, the squirrel wished them all good night and sweet dreams, but he was far too worked up to fall asleep right away. He'd always longed to be part of a real family, and now that the woodchucks and their assorted children had moved into the cave, it seemed to him they were actually becoming one.

Since it was nearly dawn before he dozed off, he slept in the next morning. He was dreaming about being a flying squirrel when something stung the side of his head.

"Ouch!" he cried, sitting up.

It was quite late and most of the animals had left the cave. Matt and the skunk had gone berry-picking with Phoebe, and the snake had gone hunting, with Babette trailing after him. Fred, stuck baby-sitting again, had been doing his best to keep himself between Margaret and the twins. So Margaret had started chucking nutshells at the sleeping squirrel.

"Margaret!" Fred said sharply.

She just giggled, pleased with her accuracy, and

chucked another shell at the squirrel. This was almost as good as playing handball with the little fur balls.

"That's mean, Margaret," said Fred. "Stop it."

"Fun!" she retorted.

The cave acted as an echo chamber, and later on, when the twins started crying, Margaret booted them out. Once more Fred almost felt like thanking her, but he knew Phoebe would never speak to him again if he didn't watch the babies, so he followed them outside. Margaret took this opportunity to start slinging nutshells at the ceiling.

Soon the snoozing Mr. Bat woke with a squeal of pain that sent Margaret into peals of laughter.

"What's going on?" Mr. Bat asked.

In reply Margaret pegged some nutshells at his wife, who soon had a rude awakening, too.

"Ow!"

This was the best game yet.

Later that day, when all the animals were back, Fred organized a cleaning detail. If he was going to be stuck baby-sitting in this miserable hole in a hillside, it could at least be less of a mess. He didn't bother the snake, who was shedding his skin in the back of the cave, or Babette, who seemed transfixed by that enterprise. But it hadn't escaped Fred's notice that the squirrel's and the skunk's fluffy tails might have been specially made for dusting and sweeping, and while he did his best to tidy things up, he encouraged them to put their tails to use.

The skunk was sweeping up the leaf bits from around

Margaret's bed when Margaret cornered her. "Funny," she said, pointing at the skunk's back.

"Excuse me?" said the skunk.

"Your stripe. Funny."

"Margaret," Phoebe said, scurrying over. "That's very inconsiderate."

"Funny, too," Margaret said, laughing at her. "No skin, just fur."

"What are you saying, dear?" Phoebe asked.

"Skin's nice. Fur's stupid."

Hearing this, the snake, who had about half his old skin off, couldn't help thinking the child was less of a numbskull than he'd supposed. But Fred fumed. How could the beast insult Phoebe after all she'd done for her! He picked up a nutshell, determined to give the monster a taste of her own medicine.

But in the middle of his windup Phoebe knocked the shell out of his paw. "She's just teasing, dear."

Fred narrowed his eyes at Margaret. Glaring back at him, Margaret had an idea. "Mud!" she cried.

"Mud?" said Phoebe. "What do you want mud for, Margaret?"

"Bowl of mud!"

For safety's sake, Fred grabbed his bowl—his last earthly possession—and took it to the nook where he and Phoebe slept. But that night, after the bats flew out on one of their moonlight expeditions and all the other animals were asleep, Margaret crawled over and managed to nab the bowl without waking him or Phoebe. The rains had stopped, but the ground outside was still nice and muddy. Margaret went to the mouth of the cave, filled the bowl with mud, and dragged it back to the nook.

At first Fred thought he was having a nightmare about being buried alive in his old burrow. But when he opened his eyes and saw Margaret caking his fur with mud, he let out a shrill whistle that woke everyone in the cave. The only one who couldn't hear it was Margaret, the sound being too high-pitched for human ears. She just clapped her muddy hands merrily and cried:

"Fun!"

"Not fun!" Phoebe retorted.

"Fun!" Margaret cried, dumping some mud on Phoebe for good measure.

This strained even Phoebe's sweet disposition, and for

a moment she considered giving the child a good pad-dling. But it would have been impossible. Since all she did was eat and nap, Margaret had gotten quite huge. So in the end Phoebe and Fred simply dragged the bowl of mud out of the cave and off to the stream, knowing Margaret would be too lazy to follow.

"Mean!" Margaret said, glowering after them.

More Fun

Food!"

Fred and Phoebe sat up in their nook of the cave, blinking and sneezing. They'd both managed to catch cold while washing the bowl and themselves in the stream late last night. And now it was morning already, with Margaret clamoring to be fed.

Out of the cave the sniffling woodchucks shuffled—one with the cleaned bowl on her head, the other with murderous fantasies in his.

On their return, Margaret grabbed the honeycomb and washed it down with the milk. As soon as her appetite was satisfied, her thoughts veered back to fun. What would it be today? she mused, licking her goat-milk mustache. She'd bounced the puny ones off the walls. She'd used the squirrel and bats for target practice. She'd poked fun at the skunk's stripes and the woodchucks' fur. She peered around the cave. Fred and Phoebe were sharing some clover. The skunk was napping. Babette was in the back of the cave, engrossed in the final stage of the snake's skin-shedding. The squirrel was entertaining the kids.

"Goo-goo," said one twin.

"Goo-goo-goo-goo," the squirrel said happily.

While all this goo-gooing was going on, Matt was playing with the squirrel's fluffy tail. Tails, Margaret thought with a gleam in her eye.

She crawled to the other side of the cave, heaved herself to her feet, reached into a cleft in the rock, and pulled out some nuts. She'd seen the squirrel hide nuts there but had never bothered raiding the supply because she needed him as a nutcracker.

"Er, excuse me, Margaret," the squirrel said, scurrying over. "That's my food for the winter."

"So?"

"Um, it's just that's where I put them for safekeeping."

The squirrel's tail was twitching nervously back and forth. Margaret lifted a foot and stomped on it.

"Yeek!" cried the squirrel.

"Fun!" cried Margaret.

Phoebe rushed over to apologize to the squirrel.

"Margaret, you mustn't do that," she said firmly. "It's not nice."

Margaret stomped on Phoebe's tail.

"Ouch!" cried Phoebe.

"How dare you!" cried Fred.

"Fun!" cried Margaret.

But not as much fun as the squirrel's. Woodchucks' tails are short and stubby. Margaret's eyes darted around and settled on the snake, who'd finally finished scraping off the last of his old skin on the cave wall. He was *all* tail. Margaret marched over and stomped on him.

"Fun!" she cried.

The snake's tender new skin was sensitive, and he hissed in pain. Then the hiss turned menacing and he coiled to strike. But, to Fred's dismay, Phoebe raced over and threw herself in front of Margaret.

"Move, woodchuck!" ordered the snake.

"She doesn't know any better, she's just a child," Phoebe said. "Margaret, you must stop this at once."

The snake didn't really want to bite Phoebe, so he just gave Margaret a poisonous look and announced: "I've had it up to my neck around here."

"Oh, but you can't go!" Babette cried.

"Wanna bet?"

"You can't leave us, snake," said the squirrel, coming up with a twin in each arm and Matt on his back. "We're like a family."

"You've eaten one too many nuts, squirrel," the snake hissed. "Look how that thing treats you. She's a tyrant."

"She thinks we're tennis balls," Matt said.

Margaret giggled away.

"I'm so sorry, snake," Phoebe said. "But you know she's just going through a phase."

"Pffft," said the snake.

Snakes can move very quickly when they want, and in the stroke of a bat's wing the striped snake vanished from the cave.

"He can't be gone for good," Babette said, stunned. "I don't think he ever even knew my name."

"I'm sure he'll be back," said Phoebe. "Don't you think so, Fred? Fred? Sweetheart?"

But Fred was lost in another reverie, staring longingly after the snake, dreaming that he, too, was escaping the messy cave and the monstrous child.

The Snake's Aches

The snake whizzed up the hill until he felt something throb and stopped to check his sleek, new-skinned body. He gaped. There, in his mid-section, was a swelling the size of a goose egg. But whenever he'd actually swallowed a goose egg, he'd felt pleasantly full, whereas now he was starting to ache like the dickens. The thug *would* step on him just when he'd shed his old skin.

The way to take down the swelling was to soak himself. He found a nice little spring and wriggled in, leaving only his head on shore so he could curse the vile child under his breath.

"Miserable monstrosity . . . human demon . . ."

But the cool water was very soothing, and as the ache subsided, so did his cursing. After a while he noticed a stone marker and remembered the skunk mentioning that Phoebe and what's-her-name's mother was buried by a spring on this hill. Could that be her gravestone?

He remembered the evening they'd all told stories

about themselves, and thought how odd it was that he'd joined in, telling them about his mother and the chicken hawk. "It must have been what's-her-name pumping me. I don't know which is worse, her following me around all the time or that monster's stomping."

But even though it was a relief to get away from the cave, he couldn't help thinking about the other creatures, and little by little the ache migrated toward his heart.

"Weird," he thought. "I couldn't really miss them, could I?"

He'd always considered them roommates, not friends. Figuring the water must be seeping into his brain, he wriggled up onto the shore. But the ache near his heart persisted.

"I must need to eat," he decided.

He slipped down the hill and made his way into the field, where it didn't take him long to catch and swallow four succulent grasshoppers. But not even this banquet got rid of the ache.

"Must be because I just shed," he said to himself. "It makes you thin-skinned and soppy."

Instead of stopping at his sunning rock, as he generally did after lunch, he weaved his way across the meadow, resolving to put as much distance between himself and the cave as possible. After a while he came to a road. He didn't care for roads. A cousin of his had once been flattened by an eighteen-wheeler.

Quite a few trucks were rumbling by this afternoon,

and cars as well. While waiting for the traffic to clear, he noticed a sign on a telephone pole: a drawing of Margaret's ugly mug, it looked like, with some writing underneath.

"Bizarre," he thought, wishing he could read what it said.

Every time the vibrations of a passing car died out, his long, sensitive body picked up new ones, and sure enough, another car or truck would soon come barreling by. Finally the sun began to set. Now he could feel both aches: in his middle, and near his heart. One made him long to go home to the cave, the other made him want never to see it again.

At nightfall, the ache near his heart won out. He even found himself trying to think of what's-her-name's name—Phoebe's sister. But homesick as he was, it would be humiliating to go racing back to the cave. If he'd had legs, it would have been like going back with his tail between them. He resolved to wait till the others were all asleep. In the morning he would explain that deserting them had made him feel guilty.

It was quite late when he got back. He stopped at the mouth of the cave and peered in, letting his eyes adjust to the moonless dark inside. The bats were out somewhere, but everyone else seemed to be asleep.

"Ugh," the snake muttered, making out Margaret in her leafy bed, berry juice drooling out one side of her mouth.

He wanted to slip into his usual place and coil up for the night—but not when that devil might jump on him while he was unconscious. He heard a rustling. The skunk turning over in her sleep. As his yellow-green eyes shifted back and forth between the skunk and the dozing brute, a glint crept into them.

He slid into the cave, right up to Margaret's ear. "Stomp on skunk's tail," he whispered. "Stomp on skunk's tail."

Margaret snored away. The snake hissed away in her ear, repeating his phrase forty times, fifty times, sixty. Finally he slipped out of the cave and found a vacant chipmunk hole to sleep in.

A Direct Hit

When Margaret woke up in the morning, she did what she always did: she sat up in her leafy bed and yelled "Food!" In spite of her sore tail, Phoebe took the bowl and set off in search of the goat. In spite of his sore tail, the squirrel shelled Margaret some nuts—though he kept his distance, tossing them to her one by one from across the cave.

"I guess the snake didn't come back," Babette said, eyeing his discarded skin sadly.

"We heard someone rustling around not far from here while we were out hunting last night," Mr. Bat said. "It sounded like a snake."

"Probably that skinny old garter snake," said the skunk. "I bet our friend's five miles away."

"Ten," Fred said enviously.

"Honey!" Margaret cried.

"Just let me grab a bite of clover first," Fred mumbled.

"Lazy!" Margaret complained.

"Can I go to the bee tree with you, Uncle Fred?" asked Matt.

"Not unless you want some stings on your snout."

"Skunk!" Margaret said.

"What is it?" the skunk asked warily.

Margaret didn't have an answer. She had no idea why she'd called for the skunk. The word had just popped out of her mouth.

But as she stared at the skunk's bushy tail, the reason dawned on her. She waited till the skunk turned to help Babette feed the twins; then she heaved herself up, marched over, and gave the tail a good stomp.

"Agh!" screamed the skunk.

"Fun!" cried Margaret.

But not for long. The instant Margaret's foot was off her, the skunk twisted herself around and lifted her wounded tail. Like all skunks' tails, hers covered two muscular glands capable of spraying musk as far as ten feet, a musk so potent and foul-smelling that animals ten times a skunk's size won't tangle with one.

She fired from both barrels.

"Yow!" cried Margaret.

Margaret had been mad before: when her brothers and sister dumped her

in the ditch in the dark, when the woodchucks fed her bugs and snails, when they'd moved her out of the burrow. But those times were nothing compared to now. Someone had filled the cave—her cave—with the most disgusting odor she'd ever smelled. She batted the air furiously, trying to fan the smell away. No effect. Shrieking, she stumbled out into the fresh air.

But even outside the air wasn't fresh. How could the smell be just as horrible here? She howled in frustration and set out to escape the stink, running as fast as her pudgy legs would carry her.

The animals in the cave were in shock, too, but luckily for them, the skunk had scored a direct hit, so Margaret took quite a bit of the odor outside with her. Still, it wasn't long before they followed Margaret's example and evacuated the cave.

"Who'd have thought she could move so fast?" the squirrel said, watching Margaret disappear into a grove of trees.

"I suppose Phoebe'll bump into her on her way back from the goat," said Fred.

"I'm so sorry," stammered the skunk. "I'd never spray in the cave intentionally. It was just instinct."

"Perfectly understandable," Fred said.

"It was neat!" said Matt. "You're a real sharpshooter."

"Smelly," said one of the twins.

"Stinky," said the other.

"Did you hear that?" the squirrel exclaimed. "Babette, the twins have started talking!"

Babette was busy pulling a leaf off a nearby hobble-bush. "We better air the cave out," she said.

This made Matt snicker.

"What's so funny?" Babette said.

"When did you turn into the big housekeeper, Mom?"

"A skunk never sprayed in our burrow," Babette said—though in fact Matt had hit a nerve. The only reason she wanted to air out the cave was so the snake would stay if he happened to reappear.

And at that very moment the snake did reappear, right in front of her. The chipmunk hole where he'd spent the night was under the hobblebush.

"Snake!" Babette cried as the snake poked his head out.

"We figured you'd be in the next county by now," said Fred, surprised how glad he was to see him.

"I felt guilty about deserting everybody," the snake said gruffly.

"The cave wasn't the same without you," said the squirrel.

The snake did his best not to look pleased. "Did I get a whiff of skunk?" he asked.

"Oh, snake, the worst thing happened," the skunk said. "Margaret stepped on my tail and I sprayed her."

"Is that right?" the snake said, slipping Fred a sidelong look. "What a shame."

"A regular tragedy," Fred said.

They all picked leaves and went into the back of the cave and started fanning—all except Matt, who used the snake's old skin to fan with, and the bats, who just hung from the ceiling and beat their wings. This was how Phoebe found them when she got back with the goat's milk.

"What on earth are you all doing?" she said, setting down the bowl. "And what's that smell?"

"Me, I'm afraid," the skunk said. "We're trying to air it out."

"Snake!" Phoebe said. "You're back."

The snake, who had a leaf in his mouth, just grunted.

"Where's Margaret?" Phoebe asked.

"You didn't see her?" Fred said.

"What do you mean? Where is she?"

"I'm afraid I sprayed her," the skunk confessed.

"She stomped on skunk's tail," Matt said.

"Stinky," said one twin.

"Smelly," said the other.

"Isn't it amazing, Phoebe?" Babette said. "They're suddenly talking."

Any other time the twins' first words would have filled Phoebe with delight, but just now they barely registered. "You mean you let her go?" she cried, staring at Fred in disbelief.

"I'm sure she just went to wash off in that stream. She'll

be back—" He wanted to say "all too soon" but, suddenly feeling a twinge of conscience, chose "soon enough."

"But what if she takes a tumble? Or crosses paths with that bear? I can't believe you just let her leave!"

"To tell you the truth, honey, she took off so fast I couldn't have caught up with her if I'd wanted to."

"Margaret—fast? You expect me to believe that?"

"It's true," the squirrel said, coming to Fred's defense. "She was moving at an amazing speed."

"A truly remarkable clip," the skunk confirmed.

"Which way?" Phoebe asked.

The squirrel pointed, and without another word Phoebe dashed off in that direction.

"Phoebe, wait!" Fred cried.

But she didn't even look back. So Fred had no choice but to scamper after her.

"Gosh," the skunk said in the wake of the woodchucks' abrupt departure. "I feel absolutely dreadful."

"You shouldn't," said Babette.

"Yeah," said Matt. "The smell's almost gone now."

"But the entire thing's my fault."

"I wouldn't quite say that," hissed the snake, with a hint of a smile.

Lightning Strikes Again

When Fred caught up to Phoebe, she was wringing her paws on the bank of the stream, not far from the fir bridge he'd used during their courtship.

"This is terrible!" she said. "My nose is so stuffed up I can't smell a thing. Why do I have to have a cold today of all days?"

Because the beast caked us with mud in the middle of the night, Fred thought. But he just sniffled sympathetically and said, "I can't smell much either."

"Do you see any sign of her?"

He looked up and down the banks of the stream. The only creature in sight was the otter, slumped at the foot of his mud slide. As soon as Fred called out, the otter came racing over, his dark eyes gleaming at Phoebe.

"You're Babette's sister, aren't you?" he said.

Phoebe nodded. "Have you seen a human—"

"Where is she?" the otter interrupted.

"We don't know, that's why we're asking."

"Babette. Where's Babette?"

"Oh, she's in the cave."

"What cave?"

"Around the other side of the hill, but—"

"Cave, eh," said a muskrat, popping out of a hole in the bank.

Before Phoebe could say another word, the otter was racing off toward the cave with the muskrat at his heels. It was a comical sight, but Phoebe's obvious frustration kept Fred from laughing.

"Maybe we can find her footprints," Phoebe said glumly.

Muddy as the stream bank was, Fred followed her along it. There were no human footprints, but plenty of others, and a fresh set of raccoon prints soon led them to the raccoon himself, washing a green apple in the current.

"Aren't you Babette's sister?" the raccoon said.

This time Phoebe held her tongue about that. "Did you happen to see a—"

"Where is she?" the raccoon cried, dropping the apple, which was immediately carried off downstream.

"Listen," Phoebe said. "We'll answer your question if you answer ours first."

"Okay, shoot."

"Have you seen a human child anywhere today?"

"A smelly one?"

"Yes! Where?"

"She was crashing around in the woods over there. Now, where's Babette?"

"In a cave around the hill," Fred said as Phoebe dashed up the bank.

The only traces of Margaret the woodchucks found among the trees were some broken twigs and a couple of recently squished toadstools. After combing every square inch of the woods, Fred suggested a bite of lunch.

"How can you possibly think of food at a time like this?" Phoebe asked.

"It's not me, it's my stomach," he said, shifting the blame. "You need to keep up your strength, too, dear. I bet there's a couple of nice juicy salamanders in this rotten log."

The rotten log was hollow at one end, and as soon as he poked his head into the dark interior, he pulled it back out with a yelp, holding his snout. Out waddled a porcupine.

"Oh, porcupine, did you see a human child go by here?" Phoebe asked.

Fred was so annoyed at having his punctured snout ignored he was almost glad to hear the porcupine reply, "Hey, aren't you Babette's sister?"

Phoebe struck the same deal as with the raccoon, but all the porcupine could tell her was that he'd heard some creature go by, howling like a sick hound. Still, Phoebe forged on, zigzagging over the countryside with Fred traipsing behind, licking his battered snout. She quizzed everyone they met. A skittish chipmunk had barely avoided being trampled under a fiend's foot. A toad had gotten a passing whiff of skunk. A huge, grinning woodchuck—the giantess from the greenhouse, in fact—had heard about a brutish creature from a little nephew of hers, but had written it off to the youngster's wild imagination. Nobody was too insignificant for Phoebe to grill: moles, lizards, tree frogs. In her desperation she even approached a rabbit. But Fred drew the line at the badger who'd taken over their old burrow.

"That would just be too painful," he said.

The milk-giving goat thought she'd heard some blood-curdling screams off to the west, but their best clue came from yet another admirer of Babette's: the mink Fred had met his first day at the big stump. In exchange for Babette's whereabouts, the mink told them he'd seen— and smelled—a human child crawling across the meadow in the direction of the pig farm.

Fred and Phoebe scoured the meadow. In the dry patches they saw grasshoppers, and in the wet parts, snails; otherwise, all they found was a deserted pheasant nest and a rusty oil can. But at dusk, when they reached the brambles near the pig farm, Fred pulled a scrap of cloth off a thorn.

"It stinks," he said, holding it at arm's length.

Phoebe grabbed it and clutched it to her breast. "It's from Margaret's nightdress," she whispered.

If Phoebe had searched frantically before, it was nothing compared to the way she now raced back and forth along the pig-farm fence, looking for traces of Margaret among the mud-smeared swine. Fred, who did his best to keep up with her, began to worry about her collapsing. He'd slyly snacked on some snails in the meadow, but he knew for a fact that Phoebe hadn't had a nibble all day.

A deep, murderous bark sent these worries out of his head. A full-grown German shepherd bolted out of the barn, skidded to a halt, sniffed the air, let out a couple more fur-raising barks, and lunged straight for them.

"This way!" Fred yelled, grabbing Phoebe by the scruff of the neck.

He pulled her toward the maple by the roadside where he'd hid back in the spring, and they dove into the hole just as the demon's claws hit the tree. While the hound kept attacking the trunk, barking like a lunatic, Fred waited for Phoebe's congratulations on their narrow escape. But she just stared out the hole and moaned, "Oh, Fred, what if that big dog ate Margaret?"

"Dogs like human beings," Fred said. "Humans feed the silly beasts—don't ask me why."

Rain had driven him into this slummy hole last time, and now, as if by magic, drops began spattering the leaves again. Soon a human being whistled in the distance, and after a few last growls the dog gave up on them and loped away. Joining Phoebe, who was still staring out of the hole, Fred heard a familiar squeaking sound behind the pitter-patter of raindrops.

"Listen," he said. "It sounds like . . ."

Sure enough, a pair of bats landed on a limb a few feet away and hung there upside down.

"Bats!"

"Thank goodness!" said Ms. Bat. "We've been hunting everywhere."

"You have?"

"Everyone was worried, so we volunteered to be the search party. We thought we heard you over this way, then it started to rain."

Phoebe poked her head out. "Did Margaret come back to the cave?" she asked breathlessly.

"Not yet," said Mr. Bat. "But your sister had several callers—a regular parade."

"Oh, Fred, I know we've lost her!" Phoebe cried. "Our poor child!"

"I'm sure she's just fine, wherever she is," Fred said.

But he wasn't so sure about Phoebe. Her breathing got quicker and quicker, then she let out a gurgle, whispered "I know we've lost her forever," and fainted.

"Phoebe!" he cried, catching her.

"Goodness!" said Mr. Bat.

"The poor dear," said Ms. Bat. "She really loved that Margaret, didn't she?"

In the gathering darkness, Fred carefully laid Phoebe down. She really had loved the child. What a rare woodchuck, he thought, to be able to love someone so horrid. He patted Phoebe's head, smoothing back the fur between her ears. She gradually came to and started weeping.

"You know, we should all be getting back to the cave," said Mr. Bat. "There's a real storm brewing."

"You go on ahead," Fred said. "Tell Babette and the others we're all right."

"Well, see you later then," said Mr. Bat. "Or not *see*, exactly . . ."

As the bats whizzed off into the rainy night, Fred took Phoebe's paw. "What you need is some sleep," he said.

"How can I sleep when we've lost our child?" Phoebe moaned.

The bat was a good weather forecaster. The rain grew heavier, and before long a flash of lightning lit up the hole in the tree. In the brief glow Fred didn't notice the mess left by the woodpeckers, only the tears in Phoebe's lovely gray eyes.

The tide of darkness rushed back in on a low rumble of thunder, and Fred moved right up beside Phoebe and gently stroked her back. After a while he lay down and hugged her.

Homecoming

A month and a half earlier, after dumping their little sister in the ditch, Six, Seven, and Eight had raced each other home. While they were out, a loud commercial had woken Mr. Hubble, but he'd just padded into the kitchen for another beer, and by the time the three kids slipped in the front door, he'd already passed out again in front of the TV. Six, Seven, and Eight crept up the stairs and into their beds.

When Mrs. Hubble came in to wake them the next morning, the first thing she noticed was the empty crib.

"Where's your little sister?" she said.

Six, Seven, and Eight rubbed their eyes and blinked innocently.

"You got me," said Six.

"Me, too," said Seven.

"Me three," said Eight.

"She must have climbed out," Mrs. Hubble said. "I wonder if she could have crawled all the way to the kitchen."

"Uh-oh, the fridge'll be cleaned out," said Six, sounding convincingly worried.

But the little girl wasn't in the kitchen. She wasn't in the house at all. After checking everywhere, even inside the washing machine, Mrs. Hubble went back upstairs to her and her husband's bedroom.

"Mr. Hubble!" she cried, shaking him awake. "Sally's disappeared!"

"Who?" grumbled Mr. Hubble, who was always cranky before noon.

"Sally. She's gone."

"Nine?" he muttered. "Well, good riddance." And he rolled over to go back to sleep.

But Mrs. Hubble didn't let him, and later in the day, after they'd searched the whole neighborhood and alerted the police, Mr. Hubble felt ashamed of his first words of the day. His baby daughter, kidnapped!

"But why would anyone take one of our kids?" he asked his wife. "We're much too poor to pay a ransom."

"That's true, Mr. Hubble. She must have wandered out in the night somehow."

"Oh, my lord," he thought guiltily. "While I was dozing in front of the television."

Poor Mr. Hubble did everything he could think of. When the police came up with nothing, he organized search parties. He and Mrs. Hubble stuck missing-child posters on every lamppost and telephone pole. But no one contacted them, and the child didn't return.

At first, Six, Seven, and Eight went around drawing mustaches on the posters, but as time passed and the danger of their little sister's return diminished, they started leaving their crayons at home. In the privacy of their tree hut, they came to the conclusion that a wolf or a bear must have found the child in the ditch and eaten her. They couldn't work up much remorse over it. Life was so much more peaceful without her, and they got more to eat at the dinner table.

For a while, they got a lot more to eat. Mr. and Mrs. Hubble both lost their appetites completely, so the children divvied up their portions. Mr. Hubble blamed himself for the whole tragedy. If he hadn't been in such a drunken stupor, he would have heard the door opening and closing behind the toddler. He gave up beer.

After a week Mr. Hubble had lost thirteen pounds, and Mrs. Hubble eight. After two weeks he'd lost twenty-five. He began to get up early in the morning again. After three weeks he applied for his old job and got it back. He could climb ladders again without huffing and puffing or breaking the rungs.

School ended, and Mr. and Mrs. Hubble made out a summer schedule. She worked mornings and he worked afternoons, so there was always someone home to watch the children. They also took books on dieting and nutrition out of the library and started shopping at the health-food store. No more syrupy pancakes and bacon for breakfast; now the family had granola and juice. For lunch, yogurt and fruit. For dinner, fish and salad. When Mr. Hubble's cousin the pig farmer let them know about a deal on a side of bacon, Mr. Hubble said: "Not interested, Hank. Sorry."

It was breathtaking how their lives changed for the better in one short month. And all because of losing their little girl! Mr. and Mrs. Hubble became very sentimental about her memory. They forgot about her howling and snatching and spoke of her in reverent tones, as if she'd been a little saint. They also spoke of her in the past tense: they'd given up hope of ever seeing her alive again. They consulted the minister of the church about a memorial service.

At dusk on the day before the memorial service, a truck pulled into their driveway.

"Dad, it's the pigmobile!" two of the kids yelled in unison.

"Your cousin with one of his deals, Mr. Hubble," Mrs. Hubble said. "Please don't let him track in any of that slop."

Mr. Hubble went out to the front doorstep to head his cousin off. But Hank didn't have a deal. He had a fat, filthy child in his arms.

"Isn't this the one you lost?" he said.

Mr. Hubble hadn't passed out since quitting drinking, but he nearly did so now. Partly from amazement, partly from the stench.

"Dead?" he said.

"Nope, not quite. Just plumb worn-out, I'd say. Found her in the sty with the oinkers. One of yours, right?"

"Well, I—"

"There you go," Hank said, relieved to get the smelly thing off his hands.

Mr. Hubble was at a loss for words. Indeed, the smell of the child in his arms was so strong he was momentarily at a loss for breath. But he finally managed a choked "Thank you."

"Don't give it another thought," his cousin said. "Need any ham hocks?"

"Um, not today, Hank."

There was quite a hubbub when Mr. Hubble carried the child into the kitchen. Mrs. Hubble let out a screech and dropped a colander full of lettuce, the oldest boy cried "P-U," the oldest girl sprinted upstairs to run a bath, and Six, Seven, and Eight hightailed it out the back door and up into their tree hut. But none of this woke the child, who'd had more exercise that day than all the other days of her life combined.

The strength of the odor helped Mrs. Hubble recover from the joyful shock of realizing her youngest was alive.

"You say she was in the pigpen, Mr. Hubble? The smell seems even . . ."

"Even worse, I know. I could swear there's some skunk, too."

It was a good thing they'd switched from soft drinks to juices, for tomato juice is the best remedy for skunk smell and there was a can of it in the refrigerator. Mrs. Hubble laid Nine out on the counter, sponged her off, and gave her a thorough tomato-juice rubdown. This took quite a while, for there was a lot of territory to cover. Since disappearing, Nine had put on an astonishing amount of flab.

Once the child was completely coated with tomato juice, Mrs. Hubble wrapped her in a towel and got her husband to carry her upstairs to the tub. When he lowered Nine into the steaming water, she woke up and started howling. "I better go work on her crib, Mrs. Hubble," said Mr. Hubble, who had forgotten the strength of his baby daughter's vocal cords.

He got his oldest boy to help him lug the crib down the stairs and out to the garage, where he kept his scrap lumber and tools. Within an hour he'd doubled the height of the crib's bars so the child wouldn't be able to get out again in the middle of the night.

By the time he and his son carried the crib back inside, Mrs. Hubble was serving dinner: codfish, fat-free cottage cheese, and salad. Everyone but Six, Seven, and Eight was at the table. The guest of honor was wedged in her high chair, looking clean but groggy.

"Wonderful," Mrs. Hubble said of the remodeled crib. "Call the others while you're upstairs, will you? It's funny, they're usually the first ones down."

The rubdown and bath had delayed dinner an hour, but even so, Six, Seven, and Eight didn't answer when Mr. Hubble called them.

"They must be up in their tree hut," Mrs. Hubble said when he got back downstairs.

Stepping out into the backyard, Mr. Hubble saw that she was right. "Dinnertime!" he called up.

"We're not hungry," Six called down.

"Don't be silly," Mr. Hubble said. "You can't stay up there all night."

"We like it up here," said Seven.

"Suit yourselves," Mr. Hubble said.

Just as the back door closed behind him, it began to rain, and not long afterward, lightning made a brilliant rip in the sky. The thunder was almost simultaneous.

"Uh-oh," said Eight. "That's awful close."

"I don't care," said Seven. "They'll kill us when the brat spills the beans."

"Yeah," Six agreed. "Better wet than dead."

And wet they soon were. The rain sluiced right through the tree's canopy of leaves. Before long, there was another bolt of lightning. The three huddled-together kids felt this one tingle up and down their spines—but they had no idea it had actually struck their branch till they heard the ominous crack.

A Good-Night Kiss

Six, Seven, and Eight leaped out of the tree hut just before it hit the ground. Terrorized, they raced straight across the backyard into the kitchen, where the rest of the family was eating dinner.

"Three drowned rats, three drowned rats," chanted one of their older sisters as they stood dripping on the linoleum.

"You poor kids," Mrs. Hubble said, jumping up from the table. "Let's get you out of those wet clothes."

She herded them up to their room and helped them into dry things. All three claimed that being struck by lightning had ruined their appetite, but Mrs. Hubble said "Don't be ridiculous" and herded them back down to the kitchen.

The second that Six, Seven, and Eight slumped into their chairs, Nine came alive. She scowled, pointed accusingly from one of them to the other, and spoke for the first time since arriving home.

"They dumped me in a ditch!"

"What?" said Mr. Hubble.

"What did she say?" said Mrs. Hubble.

131

"They dumped me in a ditch!" the child cried. "In the middle of the night!"

"Can you understand her?" said Mrs. Hubble.

"Not a word," said Mr. Hubble. "It's gibberish."

The child turned crimson with anger and frustration. She could understand them, but she'd been speaking so much animal talk her tongue had forgotten how to form regular human words.

Six, Seven, and Eight miraculously recovered their appetites.

"This isn't so bad, Mom," said Six.

"Yeah, for fish," Eight said.

"Whaaaa!" screamed the child, spitting out a mouthful of cottage cheese. "Bad!"

"You know, I'm not sure she likes it," said Mr. Hubble.

"Try the salad, Sally," said Mrs. Hubble.

The child swatted the lettuce off her plate with the back of her hand.

"Oh, my," said Mrs. Hubble. "Try the cod."

The child tried it but hated the fishy taste and spat it out. She scanned the table for something good to snatch. Nothing appealed to her at all.

"Honey!" she cried.

"What did she say?" asked Mrs. Hubble.

"I don't think she likes low-cal food," said Six.

"Well, she's going to have to learn to," Mrs. Hubble said. "How on earth do you suppose she put on so much weight?"

"What I want to know is where the heck she's been,"

Mr. Hubble said. "Can you tell us where you were, child?"

"In a cave with woodchucks and bats and a squirrel and a smelly skunk and a nasty snake."

But of course no one understood a word.

"First thing tomorrow we're taking her to Dr. Millstone," Mrs. Hubble said. "I'm sure she needs shots."

"Definitely," Mr. Hubble said. "I've never seen anyone so filthy in my life."

"Or so fat," said Seven, surreptitiously pinching the child's bottom.

"Whaaaaa!"

"Noisy as ever, I see," Seven remarked.

The Hubbles still watched TV after dinner, but now only for an hour or so, and there was no more buttered popcorn. That evening, with dinner so late, there wasn't even TV. Since Mrs. Hubble cooked, Mr. Hubble usually did the dishes, but tonight, as soon as they'd finished their fruit cocktails, Mr. Hubble and the older kids went out to the backyard with a flashlight to inspect the damage. The storm had passed, but the backyard was littered with leaves and twigs and the tree hut was shipwrecked on the ground.

Mrs. Hubble sent Six, Seven, and Eight straight up to bed. To their amazement, she entrusted them with their little sister.

"Brush your teeth, all of you," Mrs. Hubble said. "I'll look in when I've finished the dishes."

So Six, Seven, and Eight dragged Nine upstairs, gave her teeth a vigorous brushing, and put her to bed.

"Some crib," Seven said, putting the side up.

"You start bawling, fatso, and we'll smother you with your pillow," said Six.

"Yeah," said Eight, snapping off the light.

The poor child. The first thing she did was check under her pillow. The peanut-butter cookies she'd hidden there were gone. Then she tried to scale the walls of the crib. Too high. She tried to shinny up one of the corner poles, but she was too fat. She tried to put the side down, but her chubby fingers couldn't work the catch. In the end she just sat there on the mattress, staring out the window from the prison of her crib. The last clouds had blown away and she could see both the street lamp and the moon. The moon was the color of honey. Oh, how hungry she was! She'd run and crawled for what seemed like a hundred miles, trying to escape the horrid smell. She'd been stuck by prickers and poked by pigs. And after all that, she'd been given nothing but yucky, tasteless food. Yet, if she cried out, they would smother her. Whimpering silently, she thought of the cave: the sweet juicy berries, the even sweeter honey, the animals who waited on her hand and foot.

Soon she fell asleep and dreamed she was in her leafy bed in the cave. There was a honeycomb within easy reach, but just as she was about to grab it, she heard a squeak. One of the bats? She opened her eyes and saw her mother putting down the side of her crib.

"I just wanted to say good night," her mother whispered. "We're so glad to have you back, Sally."

"Margaret," the child said.

"What?"

"Margaret!" the child said, making a great effort to use human speech.

"Keep it down, will you?" said Six.

"But what's she saying?" Mrs. Hubble asked. "Can any of you make it out?"

"Sounded like 'Garbage,'" Eight said sleepily.

"Margaret!" the child repeated.

"Margaret?" said Mrs. Hubble. "Is that what you're saying?"

The child nodded eagerly.

"But your name's Sally."

"No, Margaret!" she said stubbornly.

"Well, I suppose, if that's what you really want . . . Good night, Margaret."

And Mrs. Hubble leaned in and gave Margaret a good-night kiss.

Searching

While Margaret was getting a good-night kiss from her mother, Phoebe was getting one from Fred in the hole in the tree. Even more wondrous, Fred actually dozed off with his arms encircling her. It was so marvelously calming, and the patter of raindrops on the maple leaves was so lulling, that Phoebe actually managed to fall asleep herself.

But not for long. She woke to a terrible black silence, and the terrible truth rushed into it. They'd lost their child!

"The rain's stopped, Fred."

Fred drowsily lifted his head.

"We've got to go home," Phoebe said. "In case Margaret finds her way back in the dark."

Calling the grubby, overcrowded cave "home" rubbed Fred's fur the wrong way. But even though he'd been in a blissfully deep sleep after the endless day of searching, the hole in the tree was far from paradise, and he could tell from Phoebe's tone that her mind was made up.

"Well, at least that dim-witted dog ought to be asleep," he mumbled, dragging himself up.

Once they got out of the hole, and out from under the tree, they found the night wasn't so black after all. In fact, the clouds had blown away and the moon was up. If not for the soaking-wet grass in the meadow, the return trip might have been almost pleasant.

It didn't break Fred's heart to find no Margaret among the sleeping creatures in the cave. He wouldn't have to roll out at the crack of dawn to fetch honey. Pulling Phoebe into their nook, he put his arms around her and soon passed out again.

Not Phoebe. She lay there missing Margaret's snoring. She was still awake when the bats flew off on one of their mysterious middle-of-the-night errands. She was still awake a couple of hours later when they returned.

"Any sign of her?" she whispered.

"Sorry," said Ms. Bat.

At the first pale hint of dawn, Phoebe slipped out of Fred's embrace and tiptoed outside. A faint skunk odor 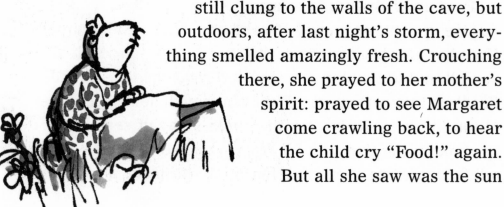 still clung to the walls of the cave, but outdoors, after last night's storm, everything smelled amazingly fresh. Crouching there, she prayed to her mother's spirit: prayed to see Margaret come crawling back, to hear the child cry "Food!" again. But all she saw was the sun poke up and glisten on the wet bushes and trees, and all she heard was birds singing.

After a while she felt a paw on her shoulder.

"You didn't sleep, sweetheart?" Fred said softly.

"I'm too worried."

"I'm sure she's safe, wherever she is. Those humans at the pig farm probably took her in."

"But what if they didn't? What if she's wandering around lost? Or hurt?"

"Well . . . we could go and find out if they have her."

She took his paw, as surprised as she was grateful.

Fred had hoped he'd seen the last of the pig farm the night before, but they ended up spending the day there, on a stakeout for Margaret.  They saw a lot of the raucous dog, and pigs by the dozen, and several cats—one minus his tail. But the only humans they saw were two hulking ones in muddy boots.

It was a distraught Phoebe who accompanied Fred back to the cave at sunset, and she nearly despaired when they found Margaret hadn't returned while they were away. That night, Fred held her tight, not even minding when her tears got his fur wet.

The next day they widened their search. They climbed to the very top of the hill to get a view of the whole country-side. No sign of Margaret. Phoebe cross-examined crows and sparrows. No sightings. Late in the afternoon, she

dragged Fred all the way to the greenhouse. But while she looked longingly down the road to town, he dissuaded her from taking it. The town was notorious for its cars and dogs.

When they straggled back to the cave, they found that the other animals had prepared a feast for them: clover and turnip greens and an ear of corn. Fred dug right in.

"This corn's fresh!" he exclaimed.

"The bats commandeered it from a roadside stand," said the squirrel.

"It was a remarkable spectacle to behold," said the skunk. "They had to fly in formation."

"You've got to try some, Phoebe," Fred said. "It's the sweetest I've ever tasted."

Out of politeness, Phoebe sampled a kernel, and she said it was excellent, but she wouldn't take another.

"You have to eat, Pheebs," Babette said.

"I'm sorry," Phoebe said. "I just can't."

But that night she at least managed to doze off.

Early the next morning, while she and Fred were still sound asleep, the squirrel tiptoed around, waking the others, whispering that he wanted to see them outside. The snake, who was still digesting a certain brown toad he'd been after since early spring, cracked an eye and hissed to leave him alone, but when he noticed that Babette was joining the others, he decided to go along after all. For the last couple of days she'd hardly paid any attention to him, thanks to the army of animals that had come traipsing over to call on her, and while this should have been a relief, he'd found himself feeling oddly resentful.

"Sorry to get you all up so early," the squirrel said as the snake joined the others. "But I'm really worried about Phoebe."

"Me, too," said the skunk. "She's so dispirited."

"I've never seen her like this her whole life," said Babette.

"I think we should help her," the squirrel said.

"Help her how?" asked Ms. Bat, who was hanging beside her husband on a sumac.

"Help her look for Margaret."

The name affected the different animals in different ways. While Matt automatically curled into a defensive ball, the snake made a gagging sound, as if the brown toad was trying to hop back out of his gullet. One little twin said, "Stinky." The other, "Smelly."

The skunk sighed. "I suppose you should count me in, since I'm responsible for the whole mess," she said.

"I guess we could help, too," said Ms. Bat. "Though, frankly, I don't think we'll have much luck."

"It's just to show Phoebe our support," said the squirrel. "Shall we make it unanimous?"

"No way I'm wasting my time scouring the countryside for that tail-stomping lout," said the snake. "And that's final."

"We can still round up a good search party," said Babette. "I can get some of my friends to help."

So, later that morning, when Fred and Phoebe headed off to hunt for Margaret, the other animals went, too— even the snake, who somehow disliked the idea of Babette enlisting the help of the otter, and the muskrat, and the raccoon, and that pushy porcupine. The search party fanned out and looked behind every rock and tree, in every ditch, all up and down the stream. But there was no sign of Margaret anywhere.

After a week of this, even Phoebe began to lose hope. No one had found so much as another scrap of Margaret's nightdress.

So the search was finally called off, and the animals

started going about their usual business. Babette went out of her way to make Phoebe feel as if she was co-mother of her children.

"They like you much better than me," she said.

But whether or not this was true, Phoebe knew she was only their aunt. She'd had a child of her own for a while, someone to devote herself to heart and soul, but that was over—down the drain. She had only one consolation: Fred. He'd changed somehow. It was as if he and not the snake had shed his old skin. Every day he assured her that Margaret was safe and sound, wherever she was. Every night he held Phoebe tight, careless of his fur.

Day by day, Phoebe found herself looking forward more and more to nighttime.

A Return Journey

Margaret was safe and sound. But she wasn't happy. The food her parents served was abominable, and every night after dinner her mother dunked her in the bathtub, and then she got stuck in the jail-like crib. And she couldn't even cry herself to sleep. If she made a peep, Six, Seven, and Eight threatened to smother her.

She began to miss the animals in the cave—especially the woodchucks. Whenever she looked at her teddy bear, she thought of the huge one she'd seen outside the burrow. For some reason, it was only now that she realized the woodchucks had saved her from being eaten up. And it was only now—now that her brothers and sisters were being so mean to her—that she realized how mean she'd been to the animals. For a while she made little effort to speak human, preferring to talk to herself in animal language. She even began to wish there was some way she could repay the woodchucks for all they'd done for her. But what could she possibly do?

One evening a few weeks later, she decided to hide under her crib to escape her hot bath, so after dinner she headed straight upstairs. When she was halfway up the staircase, her mother cried:

"Mr. Hubble, come look! She's walking upstairs!"

It was true. She was holding on to the spokes of the banister, but she actually was walking up the stairs. It wasn't all that hard, really. Because she hadn't been wolfing down so much food, she was shedding her flab.

The next evening, when she climbed into her high chair by herself, her father said: "You know, Margaret, you're getting kind of cute."

"Really, Dada?"

"Good girl!" Mr. Hubble said, beaming. "That wasn't gibberish at all. Pretty soon you'll be able to tell us how you got lost."

This was true, too. In spite of her nostalgia for the animals, she was getting the hang of human speech again.

Needless to say, this development worried Six, Seven, and Eight. With their tree hut in ruins, they went behind the garage to discuss a plan of action.

"We could throw her down the cellar stairs and say she fell," said Six.

"She probably wouldn't even get hurt," said Seven. "Her bones are still pretty soft."

They discussed various options and finally agreed on one. Since Margaret's speech was getting dangerously intelligible, they decided to carry out their plan that very night.

The three of them went to bed with their clothes on. After giving the rest of the household plenty of time to fall asleep, they slipped out from under the covers and surrounded the crib.

Six stuck a pencil through the bars and poked Margaret awake. "Listen, you," he said. "If you rat on us, we're going to dump you twice as far away as last time."

Margaret blinked, her eyes adjusting to the moonlight, and shook her head.

"You won't rat?" said Seven.

Margaret shook her head.

"How come?" Six said suspiciously.

"Back to the ditch."

"You want to go back where we dumped you?" Eight said.

Margaret nodded.

"Why?" said Six.

"Want to," said Margaret.

After holding a private conference in the corner of the bedroom, Six, Seven, and Eight returned to the crib.

"When do you want to go back there?" asked Six.

Margaret looked out the window at the full moon. "Now?"

Six, Seven, and Eight found the idea of a midnight adventure rather appealing. Eight let down the side of the crib so Margaret could get out, Seven dressed her, and Six carried her downstairs. After getting the flashlight from the top of the basement stairs they'd considered tossing her down, they crept out of the house, Six carrying Margaret piggyback.

Halfway down the block, Seven took over for Six.

"Boy, it's a good thing you've lost weight," Eight said when his turn came.

Trading off, they carried her down a country road, past a greenhouse, across a meadow, and through some trees. When they came to the edge of the ditch, Seven set her down.

"What now?" said Six.

The three followed Margaret as she toddled along past a ghostlike birch tree and up to the entrance mound of a burrow. Margaret had heard Fred bemoan the fact that a badger had taken it over, so she stuck her head inside and called out:

"Wake up, badger!"

"What'd you say?" said Six.

"Animal talk," Margaret said, backing up from the mound.

"Bull," said Eight.

"What does it mean?" Seven asked.

"Wake up, badger."

"Yeah, right," said Six.

Six dropped the flashlight in astonishment when a badger poked his head out.

"What do you want?" the badger grumbled. "It's the middle of the night."

"Move," Margaret said.

"What?" the badger said.

"It's the woodchucks' home," said Margaret. "You leave."

"I suppose you're going to make me?"

"Us."

"What'd you say now?" Seven asked excitedly.

"I said to leave," Margaret told them in human speech.

Only then did the badger take in the three larger human beings looming in the shadows behind the child. Badgers are very stubborn and strong, but their claws are more effective for digging than fighting. He could have handled the one child, but four were more than he was up to in the middle of the night.

"I was getting sick of it here anyway," he muttered, padding away.

"I don't believe it!" Eight cried. "He left!"

"You really can talk to animals," Six said, shining the flashlight on Margaret.

"Now what?" said Seven.

Margaret took the flashlight and crawled down into the burrow. The badger wasn't much of a housekeeper. The living room looked no better than when she'd last seen it, and the bedroom was still full of mud. She stuck the flashlight into the dirt floor, turning it into a standing lamp, and got a handful of mud from the bedroom and carried it out.

Eight, the smallest of the other three, squeezed into the

entranceway and started taking mud from Margaret and handing it out to the others. This way, the excavation went quickly. When the bedroom was once more a bedroom, Margaret made up the woodchucks' beds; then she carried up the splintered furniture and got her older brothers and sister to help make repairs. Finally she took the sofa and chairs back down and did her best to arrange them.

When she emerged from the burrow for good, she was filthy. She cleaned some bird droppings off the top of the entrance mound and headed for the stream.

"You left the flashlight down there," Six said.

Margaret kept going.

"Hey, I can't fit down there," said Eight.

Margaret turned and shook her head. She'd decided to leave the flashlight to replace the glowworms she'd scared away.

"Dad'll skin us alive," Seven warned.

Margaret just shrugged and kept going toward the stream, and after a moment Six laughed and said, "You've got to admit, the kid's got spunk."

They all went to the stream, and after washing their hands, Six, Seven, and Eight worked on Margaret.

"What next?" Six said when they were all fairly clean.

"Cave," said Margaret, who wanted to tell the woodchucks about the burrow.

"What cave?" said Seven.

Eight yawned. "I'm sleepy."

"Me, too," said Six.

"Me three," said Seven.

"Me four," said Margaret.

They all laughed.

"You know, you're not half bad, Margaret," Seven said.

Margaret smiled.

"If she wants to check out a cave, we'll check out a cave," Six said. "How about a ride?"

"Fun!" Margaret said, climbing onto Six's back.

Margaret pointed at the hill, and they tromped off in that direction. It was a bit of a hike, and they stopped to rest by a quaking aspen that was shimmering in the moonlight. As they were about to set out again, Margaret heard a flitting sound overhead.

"Bats?"

A pair of bats settled on a branch of the silvery tree.

"Margaret?" Ms. Bat said, astounded.

"Me," said Margaret.

"My goodness. We looked high and low for you. Phoebe went into quite a decline after you left, you know."

"She did?"

"She didn't touch a blade of grass for days," Mr. Bat said. "Wouldn't even eat clover. Wasted away."

"But don't worry," said Ms. Bat. "She's on the upswing now. In fact, she's eating more than usual."

"Oh," Margaret said, a little disappointed.

"Fact is," Ms. Bat said, "she's eating for two—at least."

"What do you mean?"

"They're expecting."

"Expecting what?"

"Babies. Fred and Phoebe are going to have babies. But come along, I know they'll be glad to see you."

Suddenly furious, Margaret stomped the ground, much as she'd once stomped tails. Here she'd been wanting to do something nice for the woodchucks and they'd already replaced her!

But the bats couldn't see Margaret's little tantrum. "Coming?" Ms. Bat asked pleasantly.

"No!"

"No? Well, can we give them a message then?"

Margaret shook her head angrily. But of course the bats couldn't see this either, and as they waited for her to say something, her anger cooled to simple sadness. "Their burrow's all better," she finally said.

"I thought a badger moved in," said Ms. Bat.

"Out."

"We'll let them know first thing in the morning. Phoebe will be so relieved to hear you're alive and well. Anything else?"

Again Margaret shook her head. But as the bats were about to take wing, she murmured:

"And say thanks."

"Excuse me?" said Mr. Bat.

"Say thanks."

"Ah," Ms. Bat said. "We'll definitely tell them that."

The bats took off, and as the darkness swallowed them up, Margaret let out a sigh.

"I don't believe it," Six said, awestruck.

Margaret looked around to see her brothers and sister gaping at her.

"She can even talk to bats," said Seven.

"It's amazing," said Eight.

"What a kid!" said Six.

And just like that, Margaret's sadness flew off into the night along with the bats. Why should she be sad because the woodchucks were having babies? Didn't she have a family of her own?

"No cave," she said.

"You mean we can go home to bed?" Six asked.

Margaret nodded.

"Great," said Eight.

"Let's go," said Seven.

And the three older children hoisted their impressive little sister onto their shoulders and set off for home through the moonlight.

Patience

The bats were always tired when they returned to the cave from their late-night excursion, but they never went right to sleep. This was their favorite moment of the day. While the other animals slept down below, they would hang upside down from the ceiling and have a little bat chat, their folded wings touching, their squeaky voices pitched as low as possible. Usually they discussed their digestion—how well the various kinds of bugs they'd caught were going down. But tonight they talked about Margaret.

"Did she seem nicer to you?" Ms. Bat asked.

"I thought so, yes. Shall we wake Phoebe and tell her?"

"No, dear, she needs her rest. Don't forget, she's sleeping for two or more."

When the bats finally dozed off, the cave was perfectly still—except every now and then, when a breeze rustled one of the dried-up leaves in Margaret's old bed. Just before dawn a splendid monarch butterfly flew down off the hillside and right into the cave, but she didn't stay long, and none of the sleeping animals was awake to see her.

After sunrise a soft rosy-gold light filled the cave and Phoebe opened her eyes. Lately, she'd been the first to wake each morning, and each morning her first thought was that she must still be dreaming. But no, she truly was plumply pregnant!

What woke her so early was her excitement and also a queasy feeling—a feeling she didn't mind a bit. In fact, the queasiness made her happy. But this morning she didn't feel queasy, she felt as if she was about to burst.

Fred was nestled right beside her, as he'd been every night since Margaret had run off. Phoebe tapped him lightly on the shoulder.

"Sorry to wake you, honey," she whispered, "but would you mind getting Babette?"

Fred sat up and blinked at her. "You don't mean . . . ?"

Phoebe nodded.

Fred hurtled toward Babette's corner of the cave in such a rush that he stepped on the end of the sleeping snake's tail.

"Ow!"

"Oh, snake, I'm sorry."

"Woodchuck?" the snake said, confused. "Gosh, I thought I was having a nightmare about Margaret. What's the big hurry?"

"Er . . ." Fred inclined his head toward Phoebe.

"Childbirth?"

Fred nodded. The snake paled and buried his head under a leaf.

Fred felt like joining him. But, luckily, Babette wasn't so squeamish. She had personal experience in such things and was soon at Phoebe's side, offering encouragement and useful tips. Fred watched nervously from a safe distance. He cringed when Phoebe let out a whistle of pain. But soon after this, Babette was placing a tiny hairless creature in Phoebe's paws. There was only one baby, but it appeared to be in the pink of health.

Fred glowed with relief and pride. "All over," he said, nudging the snake, who pulled his head out from under the leaf.

Phoebe's whistle of pain had woken the skunk, who woke the squirrel, who woke Matt and the twins. They all crowded into the nook to admire the newcomer.

"Absolutely remarkable," said the skunk.

"He's so cute!" said the squirrel. "Or is it she?"

"She, of course," Babette said. "Can't you tell?"

The squirrel was too jubilant to be embarrassed. "She's a real looker," he said.

"She is, isn't she?" said Fred.

"Completely adorable," said the skunk.

"Awful puny," the snake commented. "Hardly more than a mouthful."

"Snake!" cried the squirrel.

"Just pulling your leg," said the legless creature.

"Did I look like that when I showed up?" Matt asked.

"More or less," Babette said.

"Jeez," he said, making a face.

"Let us see, let us see!" cried the twins, who babbled all the time now.

"So what do you think?" Fred said, lifting them up to look.

"Wow!" they said.

"The miracle of birth is a truly stupendous thing, isn't it?" said the skunk.

"Yeah," the twins agreed—though as far as they were concerned, the stupendous thing was that they were no longer the runts of the cave.

But of them all, the happiest by far was Phoebe. She was holding her very own baby to her breast. She was too full of joy to speak—until the squirrel got around to asking what the child was to be called.

"Margaret," she said, reaching up and taking Babette's paw. "After our beloved mother."

Except for a hiss from the snake, this announcement was greeted with total silence.

"You don't like it?" Phoebe said, sitting up a bit to look around at the others.

"Well, I guess it's up to you," said the squirrel.

"To me and Fred." Phoebe eyed her husband. "What do you think, sweetheart?"

Fred set the twins down and stroked the baby's head. "How about Patience?" he said.

"Patience?"

The baby let out a little cooing whistle.

"What a remarkably mellifluous name," said the skunk.

"It's perfect!" said the squirrel.

"Could be worse," said the snake.

"Patience," Phoebe said. "You know, it does have kind of a nice ring to it."

"Great," said Matt. "Can I have breakfast now?"

"Gosh, the bats are still asleep," said the squirrel. "We have to tell them."

"Bats!" cried Matt.

The bats, who were suspended from the ceiling at the other end of the cave, opened their blind eyes sleepily. "What is it?" Mr. Bat said.

"Aunt Phoebe did it!" said Matt.

The bats immediately flew over to the nook. "Congratulations, woodchucks," Ms. Bat said. "How many?"

"Just one," said Fred. "But she's a peach."

"Well done," said Mr. Bat. "What are you going to call her?"

"Patience," said Phoebe.

"What a lovely name," Ms. Bat said, nudging Mr. Bat's wing. "You know, dear, maybe it's about time you and I thought about having a—"

"Ahem," said Mr. Bat. "We've got some interesting news for you, woodchucks. Guess who we ran into last night."

"Who?" said Fred.

"Margaret."

"What!" Phoebe cried. "Where?"

"Not all that far from here."

The animals exchanged anxious glances—except Phoebe, who asked eagerly if the child was all right.

"She's fine," Ms. Bat said. "Seemed rather improved, as a matter of fact."

"That wouldn't be hard," the snake muttered.

"Is she coming back?" Fred asked uneasily.

"I don't think so," said Mr. Bat. "I believe she was with other humans."

Sighs of relief escaped all the animals except the new mother. "Did she say anything?" Phoebe asked, holding her baby tighter.

"She said your burrow's all better—something like that," Mr. Bat said. "And she said to thank you."

"To thank us?" Phoebe said, amazed.

"What about the badger?" said Fred, who was interested in the burrow.

"According to her, the badger's gone," said Mr. Bat.

"This I have to see," said Fred. "Will you be okay, dear, if I . . . ?"

"We'll be fine," Phoebe said, and she started to nurse the baby.

Fred scampered out into the morning sun. It was already a gorgeous summer day, but he was far too eager to see his old home to notice the weather. When he got to the familiar entrance mound, he stopped and called in. No one answered. He swallowed hard and went down into the burrow.

It wasn't long before a very happy woodchuck returned to the cave. The skunk was helping Babette give Matt and the twins breakfast. The squirrel had gotten Phoebe's permission to hold Baby Patience, but even though the tiny thing was sound asleep in his paws, Fred was too excited to whisper.

"You won't believe it, Phoebe! The place is empty and good as new! Even the furniture's

162

fixed—after a fashion. And there's a magical lamp you can turn off and on!"

Patience woke with a gurgle.

"Good heavens," Phoebe said. "Could it be Margaret's doing?"

"It must be."

Phoebe beamed. It seemed Margaret really had appreciated them a bit after all.

"Guess what!" Fred said, turning to the others. "Our old burrow's . . ."

His voice trailed off. Nobody was smiling. In fact, they all looked gloomy. The squirrel looked positively crestfallen.

"What's the matter?" Fred said.

"I suppose this means you'll be leaving us," the squirrel said.

"The otter told me the water level's gone down back at our place," Babette said with a sigh. "If you leave, we should probably go, too."

"Oh, dear," the skunk said, wiping snail juice off the twins' snouts.

"What does that waterlogged otter know?" the snake said under his breath.

"There's more room here, Mom," Matt whined. "And it's more fun."

"Yeah," piped the twins.

"And Mr. Bat's going to teach me to hang from the ceiling," Matt said. "Right, Mr. Bat?"

"If it's okay with your mother," Mr. Bat said.

"Gosh," said the squirrel, rocking the baby. "I was really looking forward to baby-sitting Patience."

Phoebe took Fred's paw. "Do you really want to go back, dear?"

Fred looked around at the menagerie of creatures in the messy cave. He'd been thrilled at the idea of returning to his tidy, private burrow, but now he wasn't quite so sure. With Margaret gone, the cave seemed to have changed. Or could it be that he had changed? Somehow, having everything just so didn't seem all-important anymore.

"Now that you mention it," he said, giving Phoebe a squeeze, "I've gotten kind of used to it here."

"Hurray!" cried the squirrel, bouncing the baby in his lap.

"Yippee!" squeaked the bats.

"A remarkably wise decision," said the skunk.

"Maybe we'll stay, too," Babette said.

"Thanks, Mom!" cried Matt.

"Of course," said Fred, turning to the snake, "we should ask if any of the original tenants object."

"Well, it's okay by me," said the snake. "So long as

those raccoons and porcupines aren't traipsing in here all the time—and that other river riffraff."

"I suppose I could tell them to keep away," Babette said, giving him a smile.

"So it's settled then, snake?" said Fred.

"Well, I don't see why not," the snake said, lifting his head a bit. "What with all the good influences around here, I wouldn't think it would be such a bad place to bring up what's-her-name . . . uh, Patience."

And it wasn't.

TOR SEIDLER is the author of six other books for young readers: A RAT'S TALE, THE WAINSCOTT WEASEL, THE SILENT SPILLBILLS, THE DULCIMER BOY, TERPIN, and THE TAR PIT. He lives in New York City.

JON AGEE's picture books include MILO'S HAT TRICK; DMITRI THE ASTRONAUT, named one of the ten best picture books of 1996 by *The New York Times*; and THE INCREDIBLE PAINTING OF FELIX CLOUSSEAU, an ALA Notable Children's Book.